"It seems my search is over," Wraith told her levelly. "The CPS took Rachel over a year ago."

There was a silence in the room, broken only by the pulsating beat of the music, still playing in the background. With a quick flick of her wrist Raven turned it off.

"I want to know everything you've got on this adoptive family," she told Wraith.

"Why?" Kez asked. "It won't do any good now." Raven flickered a glance at him.

"Rachel never showed any signs of being a Hex when I knew her," she said. "I want to know what made the CPS find her out." She took the flat black disk Wraith was handing her and turned to the computer terminal. "And if she's dead, as you obviously think, I want to know exactly when and how she died."

"How could you find out?" Wraith asked coldly, sitting down on the dark red couch. "And why do you need to? Everyone knows Hexes are exterminated when they're discovered."

"I'm suspicious of things that everyone knows," Raven said shortly. "And, as to how I intend to find out, I'm going to hack into the CPS's own records." She smiled ferociously. "Believe me, Wraith. I'll find out the truth of what happened. Nothing can stop me now."

Hex by Rhiannon Lassiter

Hex
Hex: Shadows
Hex: Ghosts

Available from Archway Paperbacks

Published by Pocket Books

Rhiannon Lassiter

AN ARCHWAY PAPERBACK
Published by POCKET BOOKS

New York   London   Toronto   Sydney   Singapore

For information regarding special discounts for bulk
purchases, please contact Simon & Schuster Special Sales at
1-800-456-6798 or business@simonandschuster.com

This book is a work of fiction. Names, characters, places and
incidents are products of the author's imagination or are used
fictitiously. Any resemblance to actual events or locales or per-
sons, living or dead, is entirely coincidental.

 An Archway Paperback published by
POCKET BOOKS, a division of Simon & Schuster, Inc.
1230 Avenue of the Americas, New York, NY 10020

Copyright © 1998 by Rhiannon Lassiter

Published by arrangement with Macmillan Children's Books,
a division of Macmillan Publishers, Ltd.

Originally published in Great Britain in 1998 by Macmillan
Children's Books, a division of Macmillan Publishers, Ltd.

All rights reserved, including the right to reproduce
this book or portions thereof in any form whatsoever.
For information address Macmillan Children's Books,
a division of Macmillan Publishers, Ltd., 25 Eccleston
Place, London SW1W 9NF, England

ISBN: 0-7434-2211-2

First Archway Paperback printing September 2001

10 9 8 7 6 5 4 3 2 1

AN ARCHWAY PAPERBACK and colophon are
registered trademarks of Simon & Schuster, Inc.

Cover art by Paul Young

Printed in the U.S.A.

IL 5+

Dedicated to Marushka,
without whom this book
might never have been written.

Also to Peter, Tanaqui and Victoria
for being themselves.

Contents

Contents

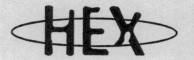

1

Hover Through the Fog

It was the middle of the night in London but two miles above the ground the city was wide awake. Lights shone in the windows of the city towers and glared in the headlights of vehicles speeding along the network of arched bridges that linked the gleaming heights. Winter was drawing in and the thick fog that wrapped itself around the towers made visibility poor. Wraith piloted his flitter between the skyscrapers with care, still unfamiliar with the complex controls, but other flitters whipped past in an instant, their occupants in search of the city's nightlife. Wraith ignored them; he was on a more serious search and had much further to travel. As he guided the flitter lower down, a holoscreen ad sprang to life ahead of the craft and Wraith blinked with annoyance as he shot through the center of a phantom image. Slogans glared from other 2D screens, flashing suddenly out of the murky darkness, advertising some of the delights the city had to offer; signs flashed everywhere, blurring into the distance as far as he could see. This was obviously the center of clubland, the signs advertising casinos, cinemas and clubs, all exclusive and expensive—a playground for the rich. The flitter was still descending slowly and Wraith was forced to concentrate harder on the controls as the network of bridges became denser, with fewer spaces for the aerial craft to pass through.

Wraith was beginning to wonder if he should have hired a skimmer. Traveling across the bridges was beginning to seem safer than flying between them, wreathed as they were in fog. Another flitter banked and wheeled around directly in front of him and Wraith had to pull back hard on the controls to prevent himself crashing into the support struts of one of the bridges. He halted the flitter centimeters away from the thick metal bar and let it hover while he caught his breath.

As the flitter hovered, the display screen on its control panel sprang into life and the fizzing gray pixels swirled before resolving themselves into an image. Raven grinned out of the screen at him as her voice came out of a speaker instead of through the transceiver surgically inserted in his right ear:

"Taking a rest, brother?"

"Raven." Wraith frowned at the screen. "How are you doing that? This isn't a vidcom." The flitter was an old model and as far as he knew the screen was only capable of showing views from the cameras positioned on the four sides of the vehicle.

"Ways and means," Raven said enigmatically and

her screen image winked. Leaning forward to look at it, Wraith realized that it didn't have the resolution of a vidcom image or the accuracy. Raven's representation of herself was schematic. Her dark eyes stared out of the screen, framed by a mass of tangled black elf locks. But the image was basic and two-dimensional. He shrugged, used to Raven's secrecy about her Hex abilities, understandable since any of them was enough to get her killed. His expression grew grimmer at the thought but he smiled as Raven raised an eyebrow to ask:

"Want me to drive?"

"Can you do that from where you are?" Wraith asked in surprise.

"Of course," Raven told him and lights glowed on the control panel as the flitter began cruising again. *"Keep your hands on the controls,"* she warned him, *"otherwise people might wonder how come you're not crashing into things."*

"OK." He nodded. "But it would be easier if you detached yourself from the circuitry and piloted this thing for real."

"I'm investigating," she said sharply. *"To do that I need to be in the net."*

"Have you found anything yet?" Wraith asked, his voice softer. The screen image shook her head.

"Nothing," she told him. *"You'll have to try a physical search. The records we're looking for don't seem to be on the main net."*

"What about a secured system?"

"I can get into those, it just takes a little longer," Raven told him. *"But I don't think this is going to be a*

computer job. It'll take a flesh-and-blood search for us to find Rachel."

"Don't worry," he assured her. "We'll find her."

"Yeah." The image nodded. *"I have to go, Wraith. There's a lot of documentation we're going to need while we're in this city. It'll take me some time to change the records."*

"OK," Wraith told the screen as Raven's image fizzed and was replaced with the normal camera view.

"Stay ice," her voice said with a faint laugh. *"You can try to drive now."*

Wraith took hold of the controls again with reluctance but found that it was becoming easier to pilot the craft. The towers and bridges were still well lit and it took a moment for him to realize that he was seeing fewer street signs and fewer vehicles were speeding along the bridges or passing him in the air. This district seemed to be more residential. The bridges widened out into plazas at intervals and it took Wraith longer and longer to find gaps to pass through to lower levels. He could almost believe that he was gliding over the ground as he glimpsed tree-lined avenues and stretches of grass beneath him. But his destination lay further on and further down. Eventually the buildings began to look less well-kept, the street lighting grew dimmer and the plazas disappeared.

The flitter sank deeper into the darkness, passing deserted levels of buildings and damaged bridges. Wraith resisted the inclination to turn up the headlights, knowing that this darkness would be home to

the urban parasites that haunted every city. He had
no intention of falling prey to London's criminal element, although it was among them that he hoped to
find what he sought. But the darkness did not continue for long. Below the flitter the greasy lights of
gangland were appearing.

As London had grown up into the sky, it had left
its slums behind on the ground. Now far below the
gleaming heights of the skyscrapers lay the urban
jungle of gangland. The high-rises were where they
had their corporations, hospitals, schools and
homes. But outside the protective inner circle were
the wastelands of the abandoned suburbs where the
gangers thrived. These levels were rarely policed,
the security services only venturing in when a politi-
cian ordered a pre-election clean-up. The people
who lived in these slums didn't have an official
identity; they couldn't get jobs or medical treatment,
no children would ever see the inside of a school.
The only way to survive was to join a gang or try to
make a living outside the law. Prostitution, black-
market trading, illegal drug-dealing—vices old and
new found a home in every city in the 23rd century.
Wraith had no doubt that London was exactly the
same.

It was the first time he had visited this city but he
worked according to a well-proven method, navigat-
ing the flitter slowly past the walkways until he
found what he wanted. The first person to approach
the craft was a boy, who quickened his approach as
its window slid down. Wraith placed his age at about
thirteen years old but his hazel eyes held the jaded

cynicism of an old man. His clothes were torn and his skin was grimy but his bronze hair was clean and glimmered under the dim streetlights.

"You looking for something, friend?" the boy asked. "Drink, women, drugs? For twenty creds I can tell you where to go."

"I'm looking for a guide," Wraith replied, considering the small figure. "I need someone who knows the city, who can tell me who owns the turf. Would that be you?"

"I can tell you what you want to know," the boy declared emphatically. "Thirty creds."

"Get in," Wraith told him, releasing the door control so that it hissed open.

"Creds first," the boy said, extending a slender grasping hand.

"Here." Wraith dug out a handful of coins from his jacket pocket, more than the boy had asked for, but he didn't hand them over at once. "Get in," he said again and, after a moment's hesitation, the boy obeyed. He was reaching for the coins almost before the door had hissed shut but Wraith waited until the flitter was back in motion before giving them to him. They disappeared immediately into an inside pocket of the boy's battered denim jacket. Wraith smiled grimly as his passenger became immediately less wary, apparently satisfied with the transaction.

"So why are you looking for gangers?" the boy asked in an indifferent tone of voice.

"I'm not," Wraith told him, and saw the wary look spring back into the child's experienced eyes.

"Hey, friend, you better not be thinking of nothing

skitzo," his passenger cautioned, his muscles tensing and a hand reaching for the door release.

"Don't try that," Wraith told him, speeding up the flitter as an extra emphasis. "I want information. If you can't give it to me, I'll let you out. If you can, I'll make it worth your while. OK?"

"What sort of information?" The boy had stopped looking ready to run but he was still tense and suspicious.

"I want to find someone who knows how to work the ganglands, who can put me in touch with the right people for a deal. Information retrieval, you scan?"

"I scan." The boy nodded. "You're looking for a fixer. But I can't get you an intro, I don't know anyone personal. I can only tell you a place, right?"

"A place is fine," Wraith agreed. "I'll make my own way after that. But make sure it's someone competent."

"The Countess is electric," the boy told him. "But she'll cost you."

"That's not a problem," Wraith replied briefly. "Where's the place?"

"Creds first. You agreed." The hand was extended again.

"Right." This time Wraith handed over a fifty-credit piece. "But she had better be worth it."

"Sure thing, friend," the boy replied. "Turn off here, you need to go down a couple more levels."

Despite a few misgivings, due to the fact that this method had not been universally successful, Wraith found that he had chosen his guide well. Kez had been working the streets long enough to know the names of the major players in gangland and, when a few more coins had changed hands, became loquacious enough to fill Wraith in on the gangs who claimed the territory they were passing through. These areas overlapped, naturally, and like anywhere else gang-feuds were continually in motion. A few times Wraith picked up speed when he saw another craft, not waiting to find out if it displayed gang colors. Kez evidently approved of his caution and the boy was quick to assert that he had no ties to any gang.

"Staying neutral's the only way to do business." He shrugged. "I pay tolls to the enforcers like everybody. Try anything else and you'll get flatlined. But I don't wear colors and I don't hang with the gangers, except for business."

"I scan." Wraith nodded. It was the same in any city. But the facts that had become clichés for him long ago left a bitter taste in his mouth when personified in a child who would be lucky to make it through adolescence.

It wasn't long before they reached their destination. Wraith let the flitter coast down gradually to rest on a wide walkway which passed the building Kez had indicated. He reached back for the pack that contained his possessions and released the flitter's doors. Kez got out slowly, watching as Wraith coded the doors shut. It wouldn't deter a thief intent on stealing the vehicle, but he didn't imagine that much would.

"Thanks for the directions," he told Kez. "Catch you around."

"I could wait for you while you do business," the boy suggested, and Wraith gave him a sharp look. He didn't delude himself that Kez had become attached to him after a ten-minute conversation. After the rate he had been handing out credits it was no surprise that the boy was unwilling to see the source of supply dry up. Usually he would have made it clear straight off that their association was terminated. But here, in a city he didn't know, he didn't make any objections.

"You can wait here if you want." He shrugged. "But I'll be some time. You can watch the flitter for me."

"Sure thing," Kez agreed, leaning back against the small craft as Wraith began to walk away.

The only obvious approach to the building Kez had identified as belonging to the Countess's operation was along a narrow spur of walkway which still seemed in relatively good repair. But as Wraith headed toward it a figure detached itself from the shadows and stepped in front of him to bar the way. It was a big man, dressed in combat gear and holding a heavy assault rifle menacingly. Muscle, Wraith realized, hired to guard the building.

"You lost, friend?" the man asked, tightening his grip on the rifle.

"I'm looking to do some business," Wraith told him, his own stance carefully nonthreatening. He had weapons if he chose to use them, but this was a formality, not a genuine confrontation.

"The Countess know you're coming?" the guard asked.

"Not yet, I'm from out of town."

"A ganger?"

"Not anymore."

"OK, go on in," the guard said eventually. "But no trouble."

"Thank you," Wraith acknowledged and stepped out onto the walkway. It was only a short distance to the main door of the building, which stood open. The windows were metal-shielded all the way up to the next level, giving the building the appearance of a fortress. Apparently the Countess was good enough to maintain considerable security precautions and Wraith was favorably impressed.

The inside of the building was dark and when he stepped inside the door he stood still for a moment, blinking to adjust to the dim lighting. He was standing in a wide empty hall, obviously designed as the foyer of a corporation building or hotel. There were about eight doors leading off in various directions but all except one were shielded and blocked up with rubble. The only empty door was protected by two guards, a man and a woman, both dressed similarly to the man outside. They stood at ease as Wraith approached, but they held their weapons with a cool confidence.

"State your name and business into the vidcom," the woman told him, stepping aside to reveal a screen set into the wall. "The Countess will decide whether to see you." The screen was dark, not revealing the person on the other end, either the Countess herself or someone working for her. The unit itself was a recent design, probably programmed to scan as well as transmit.

"Wraith," he said levelly. "I need to find some people for a deal." There was a pause before a dry voice spoke out of the vidcom.

"What kind of deal?"

"An investigation," he said into the unit. "I can't say any more here."

"All right," the voice said, after waiting for a few moments. "You can come up, but leave your weapons behind." Wraith hesitated. But from the look on the guards' faces this issue was not open for discussion. Reaching into his jacket he brought out his laser pistol, then he removed the blade from the sheath on his back and handed both weapons to the female guard.

"What's in the bag?" the woman asked.

"Clothes, computer disks," Wraith told her and the woman nodded in confirmation after glancing at a readout beside the screen. Obviously he had been right about the vidcom scanning him.

"OK, you can go now," the male guard told him and Wraith nodded. Their system was not infallible; it had failed to scan the extra knife he had not given up, but there were probably more guards further up.

The main hall had been dilapidated and dark but as Wraith walked past the two guards everything changed. He found himself at the foot of a wide staircase, the floor, walls and ceiling covered in a brilliantly reflective shielding. He couldn't see the light source but the stairway was brightly lit. He could see his own figure reflected disorientingly into infinity and found it difficult to balance with any sureness. That was undoubtedly intentional, he thought as he made his way up the stairs. They curved gradually and he couldn't be sure in what direction he was heading. However, he must have climbed up at least two floors by the time the stairs came to an end and he found himself standing on a narrow landing, staring at his own reflection in a blank, mirrored wall. His face gleamed eerily from the metal surface like a ghost: gray eyes set in a narrow, chalk-white face, framed by wild white hair.

Part of the wall slid away silently to reveal the Countess's center of operations. Terminals and screens covered the walls, connecting her to her information network. Cases of equipment were stacked around the room, all flawlessly new. In the center of the room stood the woman he had come to see. She was thin and above-average height, dressed plainly in black. Her dark hair had been cropped close to her head and the effect was one of unconcern with her appearance. She wore multiple armbands, ten on each arm, set with mini-screens and remote control buttons for the different kinds of terminals around the room. Sharp, brown eyes regarded him from a fierce, bird-like face.

"Come in," she ordered. "Tell me what you want."

"Are you the Countess?" Wraith asked.

"I am."

"I need your help."

"So you said." The Countess frowned impatiently. "What is it you want?"

"I'm trying to find someone in the city," Wraith said quickly. "A girl, about eleven years old. She hasn't shown up on any of the computer nets yet."

"How do you know?" the fixer asked sharply, her eyes sweeping over him appraisingly. "You're no hacker."

"I'm here with my sister," Wraith admitted. "She's the hacker."

"A physical search will take time," the Countess told him. "But I can use some contacts if you can give me some more info on the girl." She crossed to one of her terminals.

"Her name's Rachel," Wraith told her. "She's my younger sister. I haven't seen her for two years. Rachel was living with adoptive parents when they took off with her. They haven't contacted us since but I heard news they were in London."

"Are you planning a retrieval operation?" the Countess asked. "To get the girl back?"

"No." Wraith shook his head. "I just want to know if she's OK."

"All right." The fixer nodded. "I'll need all the information you have on her and on the couple who adopted her. Names, pictures, bio details, the works."

"Right." Wraith pulled out an unmarked computer disk from his bag and passed it to the fixer. She slotted it into the machine and Wraith watched as a blur of details flickered across the screen. When the transfer of information had been completed the fixer tapped a few keys to bring up Rachel's image.

"I'll have this sent out to some contacts," she told him. "That way we should find out something. But it's strange that the girl doesn't appear on the net. There should at least be school records."

"Yeah," Wraith agreed. His gaze was fixed on the

picture. Rachel looked like any other kid: brown hair in a neat bob, big shining brown eyes and a crooked grin. But Wraith knew it was crucial that he find her, and not just because she was his sister.

"When I've had some initial reports in we can decide whether or not to hire some people to search more actively," the Countess told him. "That should be in a few days. But I'll need a basic fee now."

"How much?"

"Five hundred," the fixer told him and Wraith nodded. The price might be a little high, but he needed the Countess's support more than he needed to haggle over money.

"OK," he agreed and reached for a cred card.

It had taken Kez two minutes to get into the flitter. He hadn't been able to catch sight of the owner's code but the flitter was an old model and it was easy to force the hatch open. It was done before the guard further down the walkway had noticed anything untoward—and there was nothing suspicious about Kez getting into the flitter when he had arrived in it. Once inside the boy cast a practiced eye over the controls. The white-haired guy had operated it clumsily but Kez had driven this kind of craft many times before. He powered up the main drive and watched with satisfaction as the control panel lit up. Then he frowned. The console's view screen was fizzing strangely although it had been working normally on the way to the fixer's building. He punched a few buttons to get an image but nothing worked. Shrugging, he decided to take the flitter up without the screen; the front window showed enough without it. He reached for the controls and froze as a voice rang out of the speakers.

"If you're serious about stealing this flitter, prepare for the ride of your life."

"What?" Kez looked around quickly, but there was no room for anyone to hide in the tiny craft. "Who is that?"

"Wouldn't you like to know?" the voice came back at him. It was a girl's voice and she was laughing. Kez sneered.

"Whoever you are, you ain't gonna do nothing on the other side of a com channel," he told it and grabbed the controls. The flitter lifted off the bridge smoothly and then Kez was thrown back in his seat as it leaped forward into the air. He was no longer holding the controls but the flitter swept easily past the buildings, faster than he'd ever seen one move before. Laughter was ringing in his ears and the voice spoke through it.

"But I'm not on the other side of a com channel," it said and the flitter went into a wild spin. Kez clung to the sides of his seat, clutching for the safety harness as he was whipped around by the gyrations of the craft. Once he had the clasps snapped in place he grabbed the controls again, but the entire panel was dead. He let go, recognizing the futility of the attempt, as the flitter came out of its spin and streaked upward through the city's levels. It was the fastest ride Kez had ever taken and to his surprise he found himself enjoying it. He whooped in delight as he sped past the hazards of the metropolis.

Then a siren went off and, looking back, Kez saw two flitters start in pursuit.

"Seccies," he warned automatically.

"*I see them,*" the voice told him and the flitter dived. The screen sprang into life to display the back view from the craft and Kez watched as within seconds the Security Services vehicles were left behind. As soon as they were out of sight the flitter assumed a more usual speed as it coasted through the city.

"That was wild." The boy grinned. "I ain't never seen driving like that."

"*Thank you,*" his companion replied, and suddenly a girl's face appeared on the screen. She was older than him, about fifteen, with a fierce grin. She bent her head in a mocking bow as Kez stared.

"You really are something," Kez said, impressed.

"*Of course,*" she replied.

"But if you're controlling this hunk of junk, where are you?" he asked suspiciously. "It's impossible. No one can do that. It's like magic." Then he tensed. "You're not some kind of freak, are you?" The screen fizzed and the image disappeared abruptly. The flitter touched down on one of the walkways and the driver's door hissed open, obviously a sign for him to leave.

Kez realized he had made a mistake. He looked out into the night. He wasn't far from his usual patch and it wouldn't take him long to get back there. But something about the mysterious ghost-like stranger and now this other ghost in the machine had caught his imagination. He stayed firmly in his seat.

"Hey, calm down," he told the fizzing screen, hoping no one would pass and see him talking to a flitter. "I didn't mean to offend you, but I never met a Hex before."

"Are you intending to broadcast the information to the entire neighborhood?" the girl's voice asked coldly, her words a confirmation of his suspicions.

"You opened the door, not me," Kez reminded her. The door stayed open and he looked hopefully at the screen. "Why don't we start this whole thing again?" he offered. "I'm Kez," he said leaning toward the screen hopefully. The door slid shut and after a moment the screen came to life again.

"I'm Raven," the girl told him, as the flitter took off. *"The guy you were about to steal this flitter from is my brother, Wraith."*

"I wouldn't have got much for it." Kez shrugged. "It's a real old model."

"Wraith won't be too pleased about you trying to steal it at all," Raven said. *"Especially after he gave you nearly a hundred credits."*

"Could you maybe not tell him?" the boy suggested.

"Maybe." Raven grinned. *"Since you survived the ride."* She winked at him. *"But don't try to cheat him again, OK?"*

"Sure thing," Kez agreed as the flitter touched down in the same spot it had occupied before. "Hey, Raven, when do I get to meet you in person?"

"Tonight, if you can find Wraith a safe place to stay," she told him as the door opened again. Kez got ready to get out, but Raven's voice called him back. *"And Kez, don't tell him anything about this. That I spoke to you, or that you know what I am, OK?"*

"I scan." Kez saluted the screen and Raven winked again before her image dissolved. Kez sat grinning back at the screen until he realized he had better get out of the flitter before Wraith got back.

When Wraith returned, Kez was leaning against the side of the flitter in the same position as when he had left, watching him with intent hazel eyes.

"Business OK?" he asked as Wraith approached.

"Yeah, I think so," Wraith replied. "Anyone try to steal the flitter?"

"Not with me here," Kez told him but felt an unusual pang of guilt as he caught the cred coin he was tossed. "Hey, friend," he said, as Wraith keyed open the flitter doors, "you got someplace to stay tonight?"

"Not yet." Wraith looked at the boy in some surprise as he got back into the car, but decided he was hoping for more money.

"I'll show you a place," Kez offered, "if I can hang with you a while."

"You will?" Wraith got into the flitter and watched as Kez swung quickly into the passenger seat. He didn't want any additional burdens on this trip and he opened his mouth to refuse when a voice buzzed from his transceiver, too low for Kez to hear.

"Accept the offer, brother. The sooner you find a place, the sooner I can meet you."

"OK," Wraith said, in response to both his sister and Kez. "Where to?"

The place Kez directed him to was a shabby flophouse deep within the slum district but not part of gangland. It was a dismal area, most of the buildings derelict. The room Wraith and Kez were given was probably better than most. It possessed three beds, made up with grubby sheets, a rickety table and chairs and a computer unit with a vidscreen. Its only window was boarded up and a second door led to a small bathroom. Wraith dumped his bag by one of the beds and Kez seated himself on another.

"How come you asked for three beds?" he asked and Wraith looked at him sharply.

"I'm meeting my sister," he said shortly.

"You going to call her and tell her where you are?" Kez asked and Wraith shook his head quickly.

"No need. I have a tracking device so she can find me." He pulled out a cred card from his jacket and held it out to Kez. "Why don't you go get something for us to eat?" he suggested, hoping to be able to avoid the boy's questions for a while. "Get enough for three."

"OK." Kez took the card. "What do you want?"

"Anything." Wraith shrugged. "No, wait a minute." He thought for a second. "My sister likes Chinese food."

"Sure thing." Kez grinned and was gone. Wraith wondered for a moment if he had been wise to give the boy the card, which had about eight hundred credits on it. But since Kez seemed so eager to hang around with him, he was unlikely to do a flit. He lay back on his bed to wait.

Twenty minutes later there was a knock at the door and, without waiting for an answer, it swung open. Wraith sat up and then leaped to his feet as he saw his sister. She was carrying a duffel bag and dressed in black combat gear and a fringed suede jacket. Her black hair was wet and straggled into her dark eyes but she was grinning as she hugged him. Wraith hadn't seen her since they had arrived in England three days ago. They had separated then, nominally in order to attract less attention but in actuality because Raven was used to independence.

Wraith, Raven and Rachel had been placed in an asylum blockhouse when their parents died. Wraith had been fifteen, Raven nine and Rachel five. Blockhouses were safe but dreary and unpleasant, and those children unfortunate enough to end up in one dedicated all their energies to escaping. Wraith had achieved this by joining a gang, the Kali, as an enforcer. Shortly afterward Raven had also escaped. Her determination to do so had become a necessity when Raven had discovered that she was a Hex. Mutants who possessed the Hex gene were no more welcome in Denver than anywhere else in the world. Regular sweeps were made of the asylums to detect anyone who showed signs of mutant abilities. If Raven had been discovered she would have been turned over to the government for extermination. At the first opportunity Raven had made herself scarce and entered the ganglands, working as a highly efficient computer hacker.

But neither of them was able to take care of Rachel. According to Raven she had never shown any signs of being a Hex and was therefore safe enough in the asylum for the time being. Later

Wraith was relieved when a couple had requested to adopt her. He hadn't imagined that they would abscond with Rachel. Their disappearance had impelled Wraith to take action to find them. If Rachel did turn out to be a Hex she would be in danger and he considered himself responsible for her safety. But it was not until she had been gone for two years that Wraith had had any leads about her whereabouts.

Raven had been uninterested in his search. The fact that her life had been in danger since she was a child had affected her personality. Wraith saw her very rarely as she had become increasingly difficult to communicate with. Her moods ranged from paranoid depression to reckless hyperactivity. It had been so long since they had been close that Wraith could not be sure why Raven had agreed to accompany him to London. But he appreciated her presence. Not only was it useful to have a Hex with him, he also had a deep affection for his sister. The fact that Raven rarely appeared to reciprocate his affection worried and angered him.

Now Raven pulled back from the hug awkwardly and ruffled her hair to cover up her reaction.

"It's raining really heavily out there," she told him.

"Here," Wraith offered, throwing her a blanket from his bed. "Use this."

"Thanks." Raven wrinkled her nose. "It's not very clean, is it?" She glanced round at the room dismissively.

"The Hilton was booked up," Wraith replied wryly as Raven started to rough-towel her hair.

"So I see," she said, her voice muffled by the blanket. "What happened to your friend?"

"I sent him to get something to eat—he was asking too many questions."

"Oh." Raven's head re-emerged and she began to comb her hair absently with her fingers.

"We should get rid of him," Wraith urged. "He's the most mercenary child I've ever met and completely amoral. He'd sell his own soul for a few credits."

"He's a streetrat, Wraith," his sister said flatly. "Money's all that stands between them and the abyss. You're mercenary too, you've just become inured to it." Finishing with her hair she walked over to the wall terminal and started punching buttons. "This is really ancient," she protested.

"It's operative," Wraith said shortly, not allowing her to change the subject. "What about the kid?"

"We'll discuss it later," Raven replied. Then she smiled and pulled out a flat package from her jacket. "Here, this is for you. Your new identity."

"Thank you." Wraith took the package and opened it. Inside was a neat stack of cards. Three bank cred cards and an ID card. The ID card had the name Ryan Donahue printed neatly under an image of Wraith; the same was on the three certified cred cards. Wraith examined the ID card carefully. "What else is coded into this?"

"You're an American freelance holovid producer," Raven told him. "Media people always look like gangers."

"What about you," Wraith asked.

"I'm Elizabeth Black, a researcher for a fictional

US vidchannel," she told him. "We can use the IDs together or separately."

"Clever," Wraith commented.

"I'm glad you approve," Raven was saying when they heard footsteps outside the door and a knock.

"Come in," Wraith called and Kez entered.

It was obviously still raining outside as Kez was soaking wet, but he was carrying two large paper bags, which he held out triumphantly as he came in. Raven swooped on them before Kez had even shut the door. He watched as she unpacked the plastic cartons of Chinese food quickly. She looked older than her computer image and less approachable. But she had the same mocking smile and her black hair fanned out in a silky cloud around her face. She and Wraith were like the positive and negative versions of the same photograph; their features were almost identical but the colors were reversed.

Raven made no mention of their earlier meeting, introducing herself only as Wraith's sister. Wraith seemed unwilling to discuss anything with Kez but Kez's questioning eventually elicited the information from Raven that they were trying to hunt down their younger sister.

"But I'm going to make some contacts while I'm here," she added, chasing a grain of rice with her chopsticks. "I might come with you the next time you visit the Countess, Wraith."

"I told her you were a hacker," Wraith said diffidently. "She might offer you work."

"That's not a problem." Raven shrugged. "I could use the credits."

"Are you going to log on again now?" Wraith asked as Raven got up from the table.

"Later," she told him. "I've got to get some rest first." She unlaced her large black army boots and lay down on the bed fully dressed. She was asleep in under a minute and Kez looked at Wraith in surprise.

"She's a heavy sleeper," he explained. "Don't worry, you won't wake her." He got up and headed toward the bathroom. "I'm going to take a shower—don't steal anything."

"Hey!" Kez began, but Wraith had already left. He grimaced at the closed door. Wraith had obviously decided that he wasn't to be trusted without even knowing about his attempt to make off with the flitter and despite the fact that Kez had returned the cred card. Sullenly he pulled a chair in front of the computer unit and idly punched buttons to operate the vidscreen. He could get only a few channels and he flipped through them several times before switching the unit off again. Raven was still out of it and Kez decided to follow her example. He didn't bother to take off his boots, crawling under the covers and wrapping himself tightly in the thin blankets. By the time Wraith returned from the bathroom Kez was already half asleep.

2

Prophetic Greeting

Raven slept dreamlessly for two hours when the sound of an alarm going off somewhere outside jerked her awake. Kez and Wraith were still fast asleep, the boy wrapped in a cocoon of blankets, Wraith tossing uneasily on top of his bed. Raven got out of bed and crossed to the computer unit. The alarm had already ceased its wail but since she was awake she might as well take the opportunity to hack in privately. She wasn't solitary by nature, although she knew that was what her brother believed, but she was wary about being observed in the symbiotic connection she had with computers. No one could mistake Raven for an ordinary hacker when she was working for real. She could, if she chose, act like an ordinary user, her fingers flying soundlessly across the keypad to perform the necessary operations. But she found it a tedious and distasteful method. Now she let her hands rest lightly on the keypad and closed her eyes as her consciousness entered the computer.

This was where Raven was now, speeding down data pathways in a microsecond. No system was closed to her and she extended tendrils of her consciousness in all directions, searching always for a mention of Rachel. Her perception of the net was not something she could describe, the way the circuitry resolved itself in her mind into shapes and colors, tastes, textures, sounds and smells. Every sense was wrapped up in the experience so that she could not explain how she knew something, only that she knew it. That was how she realized something was different when she ran into something new at the end of a data pathway.

Instantly all her tendrils of consciousness were concentrated in one place, wrapping around the strangeness to identify it. Incredibly there was resistance and Raven knew suddenly with a flash of insight that this was more than a program. It was another personality in the net. An amateur undoubtedly. The other was suffused with fear and in its disorientation betrayed its inexperience.

> relax < Raven commanded, whether in words or thoughts she didn't know, holding the stranger firmly in place. > who/what are you? < She was aware of another struggle to be free and added impatiently: > i am not part of the security services or the cps. if i were, could i do/ feel/be this? <

> let me go! < the other pleaded, fluttering tendrils of itself in all directions.

> your name? < Raven ordered, clamping down.

The other could resist no more than the locked programs that swung open at Raven's approach.

> ali < responded the other and Raven was almost overwhelmed with a flood of images that the name had set free. A sixteen-year-old schoolgirl from somewhere far above in the shielded security complexes of the rich. This was her second foray into the net and she was terrified to have been caught. Raven laughed. The girl was a novice. In a few microseconds she had disgorged enough information for Raven to trace her identity and current location while Raven herself had revealed nothing. The stranger could do virtually nothing in the net but, however inept her bunglings, she would not be caught while within the circuitry. It was more likely that she would betray herself in the real world. In a flash Raven transmitted that information to the girl, still giving away nothing about her own identity. Disengaging, Raven prepared to let herself be swept back into the net.

> wait! < Ali pleaded. Her immediate panic was dulled by the information Raven had communicated while its substance deeply frightened her. > you must wait—please wait—don't leave me! <

> why? < Raven demanded, already bored by the exchange and considering she had done enough for the unknown Hex.

> you have to stay/help me/stop the cps catching me. <

> (?) < Raven was annoyed now, her responses becoming more basic.

> because you're like me. we (you/me) are the same. <

> each of us is on our own < Raven replied. > this conversation is terminated. < And she was gone, leaving nothing of her essence behind with which the stranger could trace her. But now she knew indisputably where to find the girl, should she want to do so. Ali's signature would be imprinted on her eidetic computerized memory until she chose to expunge it.

Raven shot through a thousand data pathways in search of records. Names, dates, ages swam in and out of her awareness. School records, vidcom registrations, bank accounts, mailing lists. Nowhere could she find any sign of Rachel. But a thousand databases was a fraction of the city's computer network. She wouldn't complete the search tonight. Releasing her hold on the information that whirled round her, obeying her commands, she fell back through the net to her originating node. Releasing herself slowly from the circuitry she re-entered her body.

For a while she blinked, trying to assimilate the impressions of her senses, so different from what she had been experiencing in the net. Slowly she reacquainted herself with reality. The dark room, the breathing sounds of the two sleepers, the flat keypad under her hands and the lingering smell of Chinese take-out food when she breathed in deeply. She stood and stretched, moving awkwardly like an underwater swimmer, her body slow to respond. She walked carefully toward her bed, lying down with a deliberate precision and was asleep before her head hit the pillow.

Ali slammed back into her body and realized she was shaking. The encounter with the stranger in the network had terrified her. At first she had thought it was the end, that the CPS had found her. The discovery that the stranger was also a Hex had been almost as alarming. The feel of that other presence had been cold and alien. The stranger had been chillingly confident of his or her own abilities and openly contemptuous of Ali's. She remembered the feeling of that flood of information sweeping over her, the knowledge that the stranger knew everything about her. But worst of all had been the stranger's refusal to help her before disappearing without a trace. Intellectually she knew that the last person to betray her would be another Hex but up until now no one else had ever known her secret.

Getting up from the computer terminal, Ali walked to the window and looked out into the night. Somewhere out there was the person she had met in the computer network. Standing alone in the apartment, Ali didn't know whether she hoped for or feared a repetition of that meeting.

The lounge was a large room, furnished in zinc-white and ice-blue. Hi-tech appliances were built into three of the four walls. The fourth held a giant window of polarized glass with a serene view of the residential district. The Belgravia apartment complex was located in one of the most expensive, exclusive areas of the city. It was named after an equally exclusive region of Old London, long since lost under the developing city. Now when Ali looked at the apartment she couldn't help thinking that this was what she stood to lose if her secret was ever discovered. She tugged anxiously at a strand of her ash-blond hair, reminding herself that no one except for the stranger in the network knew the truth.

None of her friends could possibly imagine that she could be a Hex. She was pretty, popular and rich. And she was a member of the largest clique in school because her father was a well-known media magnate and could afford an apartment in the Belgravia Complex where the rest of the clique lived. Bob Tarrell owned five newsfeeds and seven holovision channels. He had a reputation for working and playing hard, which was why he was hardly ever at home. Tonight Ali had no idea if he was working late at the Tarrell Corporation or out with one of the null-brained starlets he liked to date. But even though her father was often away he was a generous parent. Ali had unlimited money to spend on holovid parties, shopping excursions and visits to Arkade, the district's recreational complex.

Now that there was less and less open land available, places like Arkade held parks, zoos, swimming pools and skating rinks: every activity was catered for. The parkland that had survived for centuries within the heart of London was now swallowed up by the industrial buildings that hugged the ground while the city soared into the sky. The ancient river was forced to flow underground to make room for the bases of the skyscrapers. With the land disappeared, the old buildings, even the medieval Tower of London, survivor of historic sieges, had fallen before the inexorable march of progress. Older people complained that the city had swallowed up its own history. But Ali, like all her friends, was only interested in the future and she intended to be part of that future.

Her chief ambition was to become a holovid director, a career for which she considered herself eminently suited. She had her future planned out and liked to fantasize about the fame and fortune she would have some day if everything worked out. Turning back, Ali turned off the computer terminal with a decisive snap. From now on she intended to use it only for homework assignments like any other kid. If she didn't act like a Hex maybe those abilities which were so burdensome to her would just go away. Ali shook her hair out with a smile. Her reflections had restored her confidence. She had no intention of letting the CPS take her away, whatever the anonymous stranger might think.

As Raven and Ali withdrew from the net, information continued to fly between computer systems. The data pathways, invisible to anyone but a Hex, spun a complex web across the city, linking it to other cities, other countries, other continents. From the most basic public terminals to the vast computer systems of world governments, almost everywhere was linked to the net. Its tendrils stretched out to encompass facilities in the most far-flung areas, but here and there were blank spots, places the net circled but did not touch.

In a blank, white room without a computer interface, or any other furniture except a plain hospital bed, a boy stared up at the ceiling. Unaware of Raven's existence, he was praying for her success, for the success of any other Hex. To the the men in scientists' coats who were watching him, he seemed oblivious of everything, including their presence. But as they readied their instruments, Luciel was hating them. The straps that held him to the bed couldn't influence his thoughts and all his thoughts just then were focused on the hope that somewhere, somehow a Hex could survive.

The long needle entered Luciel's arm. There was no anesthetic and the serum it held would keep him delirious for hours. In the time that remained to him before he lost consciousness he concentrated on the pain as the last real thing he would know. Somewhere in the distance, beyond the swirling in his head, he recognized the subject of his hatred and filled his stare with all the bitterness inside him, as poisonous as the drug that raced through his veins. But the white-haired scientist was not looking at him. Finishing the notations on his clipboard he glanced at his companions to say:

"Time for the next subject."

Kez woke the next morning to the sound of an argument in full flow. Wraith's voice was harsh and tense and Raven's cold and sarcastic but they were keeping their voices low in order not to wake him. He fought his way out of the bedclothes in time to hear Wraith saying:

"The whole point of staying here is to keep out of sight, safely anonymous. I can't believe that you would want to change that."

"Wraith, I have no intention of living in a slum

when we can afford something better. What are you afraid of? Our new identities are established—why should anyone question our moving higher up?"

"I'm not afraid," Wraith replied, his voice rising. "What you are failing to take into account is that our identities are fictional, our cred cards are fictional, everything about us is fictional. We only exist because you've fooled the computer network into believing that we do."

"If the network says we exist, we exist," Raven insisted, throwing herself down on her bed in frustration. As she did so she met Kez's eyes and turned to frown at her brother. "Now you've woken Kez!"

"So what?" Wraith asked and walked out of the room, slamming the door behind him.

Kez looked anxiously across at Raven who shook her head in exasperation.

"Don't worry about him," she said. "He'll come around."

"What were you arguing about?" Kez asked sleepily.

"Wraith doesn't want to move up into the heights of the city," Raven said, from where she was lying flat on her back. "He thinks we'll draw unnecessary attention to ourselves."

"But you don't?" Kez frowned.

"There are advantages to having a respectable official identity," Raven told him. Smiling, she added: "And I've always wanted to live in a really expensive apartment."

"Can you afford that kind of place?"

"If I tell the computer I can." Raven smiled.

"Can every hacker do that, or is it because you're a . . ." Kez's voice trailed off as Wraith reopened the door.

In retrospect it had been unwise of Kez to assume that Wraith would not be back for a while. In a neighborhood he didn't know there wasn't anywhere for him to go. He had returned to the room to attempt a calm, reasoned discussion with Raven. But the words he heard as he entered the room erased that intention.

"You didn't tell him?" he exclaimed in disbelief. "After I told you not to trust him?"

"Since when do you run my life, Wraith?" His sister sat up on the bed and glared at him antagonistically.

"You have to be crazy!" Wraith strode across the room and grabbed Raven's wrists. "This isn't about us! This could cost you your life!" He turned aside to shoot a hostile glance at Kez. "How could you be so careless?"

"Let me go." Raven wrenched out of Wraith's grip, white marks left by the pressure of his fingers. But before she could continue Kez got to his feet with clenched fists.

"Hey, man," he addressed Wraith. "I'm not gonna tell nobody."

"Oh yeah?" Wraith asked coldly. "You sell anything on the streets for enough money and you expect me to believe you wouldn't sell us as well?" He shook his head. "Raven, we've got to get rid of this kid."

"No!" Kez's freckled skin turned several degrees

lighter and he took a step backward instinctively. "Oh no."

"Cool it, Wraith, and you, Kez." Raven crossed to the boy's side and put a reassuring arm around his shoulders. She grinned at Kez. "He thinks he's really something, but he's a nice guy. He wouldn't flatline a thirteen-year-old kid, even if he doesn't like you."

"I'm not talking about killing him," Wraith snarled. "Let's just leave him here and find another place to stay and another fixer." He was already grabbing his bag but Raven shook her head.

"Don't be ridiculous," she said. "If you're worried about Kez, we'll just watch him until you stop worrying. But you're right about getting out of here. I can't stay in this skanky room for another hour."

"This is serious." Wraith scowled at his sister. "We've spent years keeping out of the government's notice. How can you totally disregard the danger of being found out now?"

"Because I know what I can do," Raven told him with exaggerated patience. "And there is no longer any possibility of the CPS or anyone else catching me."

"You're overconfident," Wraith said coldly. "And you're endangering both of us, as well as Rachel, if we ever find her."

"No I'm not," Raven turned her back on him and began to make her bed, obviously preparing to leave. "Believe it or not, Wraith, we'll be much safer out of the ganglands. This is the first place the Seccies would look for a Hex. Up in the heights we'll be right under their noses and they won't so much as blink.

They'll actually be protecting us themselves in our characters of ordinary citizens and we'll be much safer than if we continue to hide from them down here."

"This discussion isn't over," Wraith warned, but neither he nor Raven made any attempt to continue it and after a silence of a few minutes Kez left them to take a shower. He was beginning to feel that he was in over his head and wondering if it was worth staying with the strangers any longer, Raven's charm notwithstanding. At thirteen he was already tired of living on the edge.

Ali was sitting by the apartment window, drinking orange juice while she waited for her ride to school, when her father emerged from his room. Bob Tarrell was a big man, with rugged good looks and a powerful wrestler's stance. He needed very little sleep and, even after the excesses of last night, he looked relaxed and alert.

"Hi, sweetheart," he said, tousling Ali's hair. "Could you get me a glass of that?"

"Sure," Ali replied, walking over to the Nutromac unit that served the functions of a kitchen, providing meals for people too busy to cook the old-fashioned way. "Did you have a date last night?"

"I went out with Carla," her father said. "But I was working late as well." He took the glass she offered him, gratefully, and drank most of its contents in a single gulp. "Thanks, honey. Carla wasn't too happy about that, but ratings are way down again. I'm probably going to have to change the entire format of at least one of the channels. Maybe try something controversial to grab people's interest."

"Really?" Ali assumed an expression of interest. Most of the time her father's discussion of his work bored her. But as long as he thought she was interested he continued to get her invites to the celebrity glitzfests that added to her social standing in the eyes of her friends and, she hoped, would some day gain her important contacts in the entertainment industry.

Bob was still musing over his difficulties, tapping the side of his glass with his fingers.

"Tell you what, sweetheart," he suggested. "Why don't you talk to your friends for me, see if they have any ideas for the channel?"

"Sure, Dad," Ali agreed. "I'll talk to them today."

"You do that," her father was still frowning. "I've got to get some kind of hook before the party this weekend. Something to announce to people. It is a working event, Ali. They're not all coming here just for fun, you know."

"I know," Ali replied consolingly, thinking silently that for her the party would be anything but work. She intended to have a totally ultra time, playing the hostess to her father's celebrity guests.

Ali didn't have to listen to her father's work problems for long. A few minutes later a skimmer drew up in front of the apartment. She said good-bye to her father and headed outside, passing through three sets of security shielded doors to reach the outside. It was a bright, cold morning and far above her Ali caught a glimpse of the sun in a pale blue, cloudless sky. To compensate for any shadow from the towers and bridges above, the streetlighting was set to simulate daylight. As she crossed over to the car, a sleek, streamlined vehicle, one of its back doors hissed open and she climbed inside to join Caitlin and Zircarda. The door hissed shut behind her as they exchanged casual greetings.

"So, Ali," Zircarda began, leaning back against the cream seat cushions. "Tell us more about the party. The whole gang's coming, right?"

"Definitely," Ali smiled, completely in her element. "But not Carol, she's way too freaky."

"She couldn't come anyway," Caitlin informed her, shaking out her luxuriant chestnut curls. "Didn't Mira call you last night?"

"Carol's dad got dumped by his company," Zircarda interrupted. "They're moving out of Belgravia. So she won't be in the clique anymore."

"And you can't invite anyone who's not one of us," Caitlin chimed in automatically.

"God, no." Ali shuddered and it was not entirely fake. The conversation served to remind her that she could not afford to fall out of favor. It hardly took any effort for her to laugh. "So Carol's out of it, is she? Thank heaven for that." As the skimmer sped across the bridges, Ali was careful not to look out of the windows, unwilling to catch even a glimpse of the darkness far down below.

Kez sat awkwardly beside Raven, his hair still damp from his shower. She was hacking into the network, her fingers flying over the keypad faster than he would have thought possible as information scrolled up the screen. She was in a good mood, willing to explain some of what she was doing and to let Kez watch her. But his enjoyment was frustrated by the presence of Wraith behind him. He had said nothing for the last hour, and was only a disapproving presence as he checked and rechecked his laser pistol as if preparing for battle. It was a comment on Raven's decision to move higher up in the city and Kez was not entirely sure that Wraith was wrong.

He might have ambitions to live in the heights but the reality of such a move scared him. At best all he could hope for was embarrassing himself, at worst the Seccies would be completely sanguine about arresting him if he didn't fit in. The fact that Raven was a Hex made him estimate his chances of being allowed to go free if he were caught worse than those of a snowflake in hell. He also secretly admitted that in allowing him to discover that she was a Hex, Raven had hardly been playing it safe. Whatever he might think of Wraith's opinion of him, letting a streetkid know something that could get them flatlined was a disastrous move by anyone's standards. But Kez was swiftly realizing that caution wasn't one of Raven's priorities. She had a kind of reckless confidence in her own abilities that led her to openly ignore Wraith's warnings. But Kez had no idea of the true extent of those abilities and he suspected Wraith didn't either, which was why he sat uncomfortably on the edge of his chair, wondering if at any moment he would hear the sirens of Seccies coming to get them.

Raven was creating a new ID for Kez. It was in

fact the first real ID he had ever had, never having made it onto any official census records. He was amazed at the ease with which Raven hacked into the government files. Despite the fact that he had never known a hacker before, the street price for fake IDs was high enough for him to gather that this kind of operation could only be attempted by the most electric of experts. But Raven wasn't even concentrating properly, turning her head to talk to him as her fingers lightly touched the keypad.

"How would you like to be my cousin, Kez?" she asked.

"A what?" he wrinkled his nose in puzzlement.

"My ID claims I'm a researcher for a US vidchannel named AdAstra. It would be convenient for you to be related to me." She grinned. "I would tell the computer you're my brother but we don't look enough alike."

"You don't look much like Wraith," Kez pointed out.

"That's because he looks like a freak," she replied, raising her voice a little so her brother would be certain to hear her. "Rachel and I were perfect little asylum orphans but everyone looked askance at Wraith. It's ironic that he's never shown the slightest sign of being a Hex, despite the fact that he looks about as freaky as you can get."

"Wraith looks like a ganger," Kez said, trying to smooth things over. "It's not really freaky, just scary." He bit his lip, thinking of the gangers he had been unfortunate enough to know, but Raven just laughed.

"That's ironic as well. I'm much more frightening than Wraith," she told him, then glanced back at the computer before he could attempt a reply. "OK, I'm done here. Would you like to know your new name?"

"It's not anything weird, is it?" Kez asked, mistrusting Raven's sense of humor.

"Would I do that?" Raven asked facetiously. "No, it's as close to your real name as I could make it. You are now Kester Chirac, a Canadian national. You flew over from San Francisco last week, traveling executive class, seat 14C. Your cousin, Elizabeth Black, had seat 14B. AdAstra's research department paid for both fares—media people are expected to scam their company for their family's benefit."

"Is that really all in the records?" Kez asked in astonishment.

"And a lot more." Raven leaned back in her chair with a self-satisfied expression. "Do you want to know about the flitter that took you from the airport to London, or the hotel you stayed in last week?" She leaned forward again, sweeping her hands across the keypad. "There's your hotel bill at the Regent."

Kez stared at the screen in fascination and was aware that Wraith had come up behind them and was looking as well.

"It's a large bill for just a week," he commented.

"Kez charged a lot to room service," Raven said dryly and Kez realized with relief that they were reconciled again.

"When did I check out?" he asked, studying the lines of type.

"Tomorrow," Raven told him. "When we move into our apartment."

"And where is this apartment?" Wraith asked, his voice impassive.

"The Belgravia Complex." Raven shrugged. "It's full of media people, null-brainers and phoneys. But I guess we can stand it for a while."

"Electric!" Kez said under his breath. He had decided that, whatever the risk, he wasn't about to get separated from his newfound companions just yet.

3

Strange Matters

Raven and Kez moved into the Belgravia Complex the next afternoon in style. Wraith had gone to find the Countess, unwilling to participate in arranging for an apartment, an action he hadn't condoned, so they went ahead without him. The apartment Raven had rented at an astronomical price was luxurious in the extreme, and the furnishings that arrived in a huge transit a few minutes after their flitter pulled up outside the complex were equally so. According to Raven, the apartment had originally been fitted out in pale pastels but, unbeknownst to Wraith, she had ordered decorators to refit it according to her specifications.

As the people from the furnishing company moved their new possessions into the apartment, Kez began to get quite a comprehensive idea of what Raven's preferences were. Apparently she favored dark colors, particularly deep crimson and russet-brown. She also liked loud music. Technicians were

rewiring the apartment's music system to accom-
modate the industrial-strength megawatt speakers
Raven had requested, and the first thing she did
when the furnishings were moved in was to call up a
music company and order what sounded like half
their listings. Kez hadn't heard of any of it but, when
the lasdisks began to stack up in the lounge, he privately decided it was ganger-style music. Some was
relatively recent, jetrock and acidtechno, but there
were reissues from way back in the late 20th century
with the most dismal and depressing lyrics he had
ever heard.

"It's *fin de siècle* music," Raven told him, when he
protested. "It's got realism. Those musicians saw the
deluge coming and they weren't afraid to say so,
when the politicians were too scared to admit it."

"What are you talking about?" Kez asked, strain-
ing to be heard over the crashing backbeats of the
sound system.

"The technological age," Raven replied, turning
the music down a fraction in consideration for his
ringing ears. "The loss of history in the march of
progress. How do you think the genetics experiments
came about? Throughout the whole of the 21st century, scientists tried to improve people to bring them
into line with the new technology. Science took over
the world—that's how come London shot three kilometers into the sky." She laughed, as she flipped
through the assortment of disks. "The only reason it
isn't even higher was that the cities slowed down a bit
after the crash of New York; and they'd reached five
kilometers before the supports gave way."

"Could that happen here?" Kez asked, alarmed for the first time in his life about the city's stability.

"No chance." Raven grinned at his expression. "New alloys, new building techniques. Terrorists tried to blow up LA in 2314 and couldn't do any more than smash a few bridges. The skyrises are here to stay."

Raven wasn't really in a mood for conversation and Kez could only stand so much of the thumping music. Leaving her to play with the system, he went out to explore the complex, armed with the fake IDs that had arrived by registered courier as they moved in. With an account balance of 800 credits Kez was ready to sample some of Belgravia's much vaunted facilities.

The experience left him bewildered. He had flagged down a skimmer to take him to the rec complex and it blew his mind. He had never seen so much space devoted to recreation. Arkade had areas he hadn't even heard of. He had no idea how to ice skate and he stared at the glittering expanse of frozen water in incomprehension. And he was even puzzled by the museum. Kez couldn't imagine why anyone would want to look at carved rocks and pictures of dead people they didn't even know. But it was full of old people, looking at the stuff with evident fascination. In the end he followed a group of kids, a couple of years older than him, who had just got out of school. He tailed them around for about half an hour as they checked out music and clothes stores; eventually buying some viddisks he thought Raven might like because he couldn't think what else to get and was worried about being stopped by a store cop. He was looking at a synthleather jacket, wondering if he should get rid of his old denim one, when he noticed one of the girls in the group he had been following standing next to him.

She flashed him a brilliant smile as he turned to look at her and held out a smooth hand. He took it, more out of surprise than anything else, as she introduced herself.

"I'm Zircarda Anthony—my parents run the Anthony Corporation," she told him. "You must be new to Belgravia, right?"

"I'm Kez, Kester Chirac," he added. "I just moved in today."

"Are you going to go to Gateshall?" Zircarda asked. "We all do." She waved airily at the rest of her group of friends.

"That's a school, isn't it?" Kez said, alarmed at the possibility and wondering why this girl was asking him so many questions. "No, I don't think so." The girl looked surprised and he lied quickly, his instincts taking over. "I go to school back in the States. I've come over with my cousin—she's a researcher for a vidchannel."

"What channel?" a girl with ash-blond hair asked authoritatively.

"AdAstra," Kez replied, desperately trying to remember the cover story Raven had primed him with.

"I haven't heard of it," the second girl said superciliously and a third, this one with curly brown hair, informed him:

"Ali's father owns seven vidchannels."

"Really?" Kez's heart sank and he wondered how he was going to get out of this one. The answer came to him just as he was getting desperate. "AdAstra's kind of alternative. It's into 20th-century music, kind of *fin de siècle*." He was pretty sure that he had pronounced the last phrase wrong, but it looked as if the girls had accepted it.

"I knew you would be into alternative music as soon as I saw you," Zircarda pronounced triumphantly. "You know your jacket makes you look just like a ganger."

"Yeah," Kez replied, too astonished to think what else to say. But the group of kids talked enough for it not to matter. Zircarda introduced them all, with brief explanations attached.

"This is Ali, Bob Tarrell's daughter, and Caitlin, her father's an MP, and Mira, her mother is Martia West the actress . . ." The list went on and on as Kez was presented to each and every member of a group of kids who apparently thought of themselves as a kind of exclusive gang for the children of the very rich.

Within minutes Zircarda had extracted from him the location of the apartment Raven had rented and his "cousin's" name, and had quizzed him in detail about *fin de siècle* rock. He was completely terrified at what Wraith might say when he found out about this and worried that any minute he would get tangled up in his own lies. Eventually he got away, claiming his cousin was expecting him back, and flagged down a fast flitter outside Arkade to take him back to the apartment.

*　　*　　*

As it happened, Kez had no chance to explain what had gone on at the rec complex. He arrived back at the apartment only seconds after Wraith, who was as excited as the boy had ever seen him. Raven had actually turned off the screeching music in order to listen to what he was saying.

"The Countess has found Rachel's adoptive parents," he announced as Kez walked in the door. "One of her contacts recognized their pictures, some ganger who works the area. They've changed their names, which was why we couldn't find them."

"What about Rachel?" Raven asked.

"Nothing." Wraith's face clouded over a little. "The person who recognized them didn't remember having seen her. But he said they had two kids."

"That's great!" Kez said enthusiastically, inwardly wondering if Raven and Wraith would dump him as soon as they found their sister. "Are you going to find them now?"

"Let me check them out in the nets instead," Raven suggested. Kez was surprised at this uncharacteristic display of caution but Wraith's reaction was one he couldn't have anticipated.

"Instead?" he stared piercingly at Raven. "Don't you want to see Rachel?"

"I came to London with you, didn't I?" Raven bristled, taking umbrage at her brother's tone. "I'm just not as obsessed with this thing as you are, OK?"

"This isn't obsession." Wraith shook his head. "You just have no idea, do you, Raven? You can't relate to other people at all, just machinery." His gray eyes were as hard as ice and Raven stared back at him, white with rage. She was too angry even to speak. Swinging around, she headed for one of the bedrooms, slamming the door behind her with a crash.

Kez stared after her in alarm, then turned to look at Wraith, utterly astonished.

"It sounded like you hate her," he said in amazement.

"I don't know Raven very well anymore," Wraith said stiffly. "When she stops sulking, tell her I've gone to find Rachel." Kez only hesitated for a moment.

"I'm coming with you," he told Wraith.

"I don't recall inviting you," Wraith said coldly.

"Oh no." Kez shook his head. "You're not leaving me behind now. You got her into this mood—I don't want to be here until she gets out of it."

"Come on then," Wraith said shortly and headed for the door. Kez followed him as quickly as he could. But they had barely reached the flitter when they heard the music starting up behind them, even louder than before.

As he strapped himself into the passenger seat of the flitter Kez wondered if he should have told Raven about his encounter with the Gateshall clique in the mall. But the thudding noise he could hear even with the flitter's doors shut warned him against returning to the apartment. As Wraith took off, Kez settled himself more comfortably in his seat, hoping that in subjecting herself to that atonal din Raven would work herself back into a reasonable mood.

*   *   *

When the group left Arkade, Zircarda and Caitlin went back with Ali to her apartment. By the time they had stretched out in the lounge in front of the vidscreen, Ali and Caitlin were bored by the thought of Elizabeth Black and Kester Chirac. However, Zircarda had decided Kez was an original: dressing like a ganger but too young to be a genuine threat. A new addition to Belgravia was always an event since the complex attracted some of the richest and most influential people in the city. Knowing the new arrivals before anyone else would add to Zircarda's social standing and, through Kez, she would be bound to be one of the first to meet Elizabeth. If anyone else had gone on in this way Ali and Caitlin would have absented themselves. After all, Zircarda had only met a weird kid at least three years younger than them. But Zircarda was the undisputed leader of their clique and they listened patiently, agreeing whenever Zircarda paused for breath.

She finally wound to a standstill in the middle of UltraX's chart show, which Ali and Caitlin had been watching with half an eye as they listened to her, when Bob Tarrell came in the front door of the apartment.

"Dad, what are you doing home?" Ali asked in surprise.

"I need to work on the arrangements for the party, honey," he replied, already heading for his study. "Try and keep it down in here, kids, OK?"

"Sure, Dad," Ali said and turned back to see Zircarda regarding her with an expression she had come to recognize. The brilliant smile, coupled with the calculating look in her eyes, could only mean that her friend wanted something.

"Hey, Ali," Zircarda began, with a casual air. "What do you think of inviting Kez and his cousin to your party?"

"I don't know if my Dad would be keen on me inviting any more of my friends," Ali replied uneasily. "He keeps saying that it's supposed to be for work." Zircarda's expression began to change and Caitlin leaped in quickly before things could get uncomfortable:

"Ali, didn't you tell us yesterday that your Dad wants to change the format of one of his channels, and that he needs ideas?"

"Yes, I did," Ali replied slowly.

"Well, Kez's cousin works for an alternative rock channel—maybe she would have some ideas," Caitlin suggested, glancing at Zircarda for approval. She got it.

"And if your father invites Kez's cousin, we can introduce her to everybody!" she proclaimed triumphantly. Ali knew when she was beaten.

"I'll ask him when he next stops for a break," she said. "He'll just be mad if I disturb him now."

"OK," Zircarda agreed, allowing the minor point now that she had got her own way again. "This party's going to be the most!"

The flitter pulled up on a tree-lined bridge in a quiet residential district. It was not as luxurious as the Belgravia Complex, but Kez thought it looked nice, attractive and peaceful. As they got out of the flitter he felt out of place in a way he hadn't in Belgravia. Wraith looked forbidding enough in his black leathers, and Kez felt as if anyone could tell at a glance that he was just a streetrat. When Wraith locked up the flitter he didn't move from its side.

"What's the matter?" Wraith asked.

"I shouldn't be here," Kez said gruffly. "I don't fit in."

"Snap out of it," Wraith told him. Then, when Kez didn't move, he rested a hand lightly on his shoulder. "Come on, kid," he said quietly. "No one here knows anything about you."

"I'm not one of them," Kez hissed. "I want to stay in the flitter."

"I'm not going to leave you here," Wraith informed him and Kez clenched his fists.

"I'm not going to steal it, Wraith," he glared furiously. Then he deflated. "But I almost did, when you first picked me up. Raven wouldn't let me. You were right about me, weren't you? You can't trust anyone who lives on the streets!" He turned away, not wanting Wraith to look at him.

"Kez." Wraith slung an arm on his shoulders. "Calm down."

"Why don't you just get rid of me now?" Kez replied bitterly. "You'll do it anyway, just as soon as you find your sister."

"No I won't," Wraith replied seriously. He turned Kez to face him. "You really don't know anything about me, Kez," he said. "And you definitely don't know anything about Raven." He shook his head. "She attached you on a whim, Kez, and she could just as easily dump you again, probably without thinking twice about it." He frowned. "But you needn't worry about what'll happen when we leave. I'll make sure you won't have to go back to the streets." He sighed. "I might not trust you, Kez, and I know you don't like me very much. But I was a ganger for a long time, and the Kali always took care of their own." He took Kez's arm firmly, forcing him to walk off down the bridge with him. "Now, come on. I don't want to waste any time."

Kez fell into step with him obediently, wondering if he had misjudged Wraith. It was a few minutes before he could trust himself to speak.

"Do you still run with them, your gang?"

"No." Wraith shook his head. "We parted company about a year ago. I was tired of being on the wrong side of the law at the time."

"But Raven wasn't?"

"Raven's existence puts her on the wrong side of the law to start off with," Wraith said. "She's never cared very much for conventional morality." He didn't look at Kez as he added: "We haven't been close for a long time, but I've heard a lot about her from friends of mine. She's not really normal, Kez. In more ways than one."

"Oh." Kez was silent again. Not really knowing what to say, he decided to ask a question that had been bugging him since he first met them. "Are those your real names?" he asked. "Wraith and Raven."

"No." Wraith smiled, for the first time since Kez had met him. "Raven probably wouldn't be too pleased if I told you her real name. I think I'm the only one who remembers it. She's expunged all records of her original identity from the net. But mine is, was, Rhys. The Kali called me Wraith because of my hair."

"And your skin, and your eyes," Kez added, beginning to regain his confidence.

"As you say." Wraith nodded. "Raven chose her own name. She has quite a reputation back in Denver."

"Not a good one, huh?" Kez asked.

"No," Wraith said grimly. Then he came to a halt outside one of the towers. "This is it. Three floors up."

"I hope you find your sister," Kez said, as they entered the building. "You must really miss her."

"I'm responsible for her," Wraith replied, a little sternly. Then he added: "But yes, I miss her as well."

The apartment they wanted was numbered 37 and when Wraith touched the call signal beside the door it opened almost immediately. The woman who opened it was middle-aged and dressed conservatively. She regarded Wraith and Kez a little dubiously but seemed reassured by Wraith's polite tone of voice.

"Mrs. Hollis?" he asked.

"Yes?" she replied.

"I wonder if I could speak to you for a moment?" Wraith said. "It's quite important."

"Well, all right." The woman opened the door just wide enough for them to enter and Kez followed Wraith into a plainly decorated room. Two little girls with blond hair tied up in ribbons, aged about six, were seated in front of the vidscreen, watching an animation.

"Camilla, Tamara, go and play in your room," the woman told them. "Don't argue," she added sharply, "you can watch the screen any time." Kez watched as the little girls got up and left. He remembered Wraith saying that Rachel's adoptive parents were known to have only two children, and he wondered if the Countess had made a mistake. If these were the kids where was Rachel?

Wraith was looking grim again, his eyes troubled. But he thanked the woman politely as she invited him to sit down.

"Mrs. Hollis," he said, once she had seated herself facing them. "Am I correct in believing that you and your husband adopted a child six years ago in Denver, under the names Vanessa and Carl Michaelson?"

"Oh my god," Mrs. Hollis whispered, the color draining from her face. "What do you want?"

"I'm not here to cause any trouble," Wraith said quietly. "But the child you adopted was my sister, Rachel. I just want to know that she's all right." Kez knew the answer before Mrs. Hollis spoke—nothing good could come out of fear like that.

"I'm sorry," she said, standing up. "Please leave. I can't tell you anything."

"Mrs. Hollis." Wraith stood up as well and faced her. He was several inches taller and she seemed to shrink before him. "I'm afraid I can't leave until you give me some answers. Rachel obviously isn't here. What happened to her? Is she even still alive?"

"I don't know," the woman said hoarsely. "I swear to you, I don't know. They came and took her. She's not here anymore."

"Who, who took her?" Wraith demanded.

"The CPS," Mrs. Hollis told him, leaning back against her chair. "Over a year ago. They said a mutation had shown up in her medical examination." Her eyes were clouded with unshed tears. "I'm sorry," she said. "I can't have children of my own. Rachel was just like my own daughter. Please don't tell anyone I told you all this. The CPS operatives said we shouldn't mention it to anyone. If the Security Services find out I've spoken to you they could take the twins away. I don't know what I'd do if I lost them."

"I said I wasn't here to cause you any trouble," Wraith replied. "Thank you for telling me the truth." He turned to leave. "Come on, Kez, let's go. There's nothing more for us to do here." Wraith keyed the door open and Kez followed him out. As they left, Mrs. Hollis watched them go, a pathetic crumpled figure sitting on the arm of the chair.

Wraith didn't stop walking until they had left the building far behind. Then he came to a halt at the beginning of the bridge where they had left the flitter. He looked over, gazing down through the hundreds of levels of the city, saying nothing. Kez didn't know what to say. Everyone knew that the CPS coming for someone was a death sentence. Wraith had just heard evidence that his sister was dead, after searching for her for four years.

"I'm sorry," he said quietly.

"I know." Wraith stared down into the darkness of the depths far below. "Raven said Rachel wasn't a Hex," he said after a while. Kez was silent. A few minutes passed slowly before he wondered if Wraith wanted to be alone. He was about to back away when Wraith spoke:

"Just give me a minute," he said, glancing up. "I have to think."

"OK," Kez replied and leaned against the balustrade next to Wraith. He assumed that the ganger was coming to terms with his failure. Flitters passed overhead and skimmers moved behind them on the bridge, but neither of them spoke again for some time.

Bob Tarrell could hear the music pounding as he walked up to the apartment. He recognized the wail of an electric guitar somewhere in the cacophony but the rest of the music was as dissonant as anything he'd ever heard. However, he didn't allow that to faze him as he put his hand to the black metal plate by the door. When there was no answer he pressed it again. Eventually a voice came out of the wall speaker:

"Who is it ?"

"I'm Bob Tarrell, of the Tarrell media corporation," he told it, looking up at the security camera. Its light was turned on even though no image had appeared on the screen facing him. "I live in the Complex." He waited a while and was about to speak again when the main door of the apartment slid smoothly open.

A girl was standing there. She was dressed in black, the color complementing her stark black hair and her black eyes, dark against her pale face. She was frowning as she looked at him.

"Have you come to complain about the music?" she asked, before he could speak.

"Definitely not," he assured her. Then he extended his hand. "You must be Elizabeth Black. My daughter knows your cousin."

"She does?" The girl raised her eyebrows, then abruptly smiled, taking his hand in a firm grasp. "I'm sorry, Mr. Tarrell. Please, come in."

Inside she took a moment to key the music down to a barely audible hum and offered him a drink. He accepted the offer of sake and the girl collected two cups from the Nutromac, handing one to him.

"I'm very pleased to meet you, Mr. Tarrell," she told him. "Your corporation pretty much dominates the British media, and maintains a presence in the European Federation in general, I believe."

"You flatter me, Miss Black," Bob smiled. "It will be a while yet before the Tarrell corporation makes a real name for itself in Europe."

"Elizabeth, please," she told him, and he nodded.

"Elizabeth, I hear that you're a researcher for a US vidchannel. My daughter's friends met your cousin this afternoon at Arkade."

"News travels quickly," the girl replied, flashing him a quick grin.

"It does in the Belgravia Complex," Bob smiled back. "And, seeing as we're in the same business, I was naturally interested. I'm afraid I haven't heard of AdAstra before though."

"It's still only a small channel," she replied smoothly. "But we hope to move on to bigger things. One of the reasons Kez and I are here is to investigate the possibility of a British connection. Do you think your corporation would be interested?"

"Perhaps," Bob replied cautiously. "I'd certainly be interested in discussing it with you. But I'm not quite sure how well your style would succeed in Britain."

"Ah, yes." The girl stretched like a cat and studied him with dark, unreadable eyes. "How much do you know about my channel, Mr. Tarrell?"

"Only that it's centered on alternative rock of the late 20th century. My daughter couldn't tell me much more. But even that seems a pretty radical approach."

"In the present climate, the more radical a channel is, the better," she stated seriously. "And AdAstra's following, although small, is very devoted." She gestured at the stacks of lasdisks in the lounge. "This kind of music has a cult status. The mood of the late 20th century was very dark and its music reflects that. A lot of people find it very addictive."

"You are obviously one of them," he said and Elizabeth inclined her head slightly in assent. "I think I'd like to know more about your channel," he told her. "And particularly about this music."

Bob Tarrell had intended to stay for only about fifteen minutes. He ended up staying for over an hour. During that time, Elizabeth had played him several tracks from her vast selection and given him a comprehensive induction into 20th-century music. Of everything she told him it was the expression "cult" that had interested him the most. Alternative music with a cult status would be a new departure for him, but it was the kind of thing that might generate the interest he needed in his failing channel. By the time he finally left Elizabeth's apartment he had already decided how he would alter its format, with the help of AdAstra's young researcher. And he had invited both Elizabeth and her cousin to his get-together that weekend. He was almost certain that, by then, she would be his star guest.

Kez realized that something must have occurred to calm Raven down by the time he and Wraith got back to the apartment. The music was no longer painfully audible, and was playing at an acceptable level as they entered the door. Raven had been watching the vidscreen but she looked up as they came in. She looked as if she was gearing herself up to be angry again, but her expression changed as she saw Wraith's face.

"What happened?" she asked in surprise.

"The CPS took Rachel over a year ago," Wraith told her levelly. "It seems my search is over."

There was a silence in the room, broken only by the pulsating beat of the music, still playing in the background. With a quick flick of her wrist Raven turned it off.

"I want to know everything you've got on this adoptive family," she told Wraith.

"Why?" Kez asked. "It won't do any good now." Raven flickered a glance at him.

"Rachel never showed any signs of being a Hex when I knew her," she said. "I want to know what made the CPS find her out." She took the flat black disk Wraith was handing her and turned to the computer terminal. "And if she's dead, as you obviously think, I want to know exactly when and how she died."

"How could you find out?" Wraith asked coldly, sitting down on the dark red couch. "And why do you need to? Everyone knows Hexes are exterminated when they're discovered."

"I'm suspicious of things that everyone knows," Raven said shortly. "And, as to how I intend to find out, I'm going to hack into the CPS's own records." She smiled ferociously. "Believe me, Wraith. I'll find out the truth of what happened. Nothing can stop me now."

4

Fatal Entrance

Raven sank into the computer like a swimmer into the sea, immersing herself in the electronic labyrinth. It was a maze to which only she had the key and she moved through it like a goddess, contemptuous of the pathetic attempts of human users to fathom its fascinating complexities. It was easy for her to be seduced by the glowing trails of information pathways, leading away from her in all directions, but she concentrated on the focus of her search—the name Rachel Hollis.

Raven did not move straight to the CPS's databases. Despite her confidence, she as yet had no idea how she would find those records. So her first action was to stream down the net toward the computer system of the British government. This was one of the most impressively shielded systems in the country, but no computer could hope to be secure from Raven. However, it put up an amusing resistance. As she entered the system an automatic watchdog program intercepted her.

> **request authorization please?** < it demanded.

> **correct authorization submitted—doubleplus priority user** < Raven informed it, snowing it with information. She had penetrated this system many times before and the challenge was decreasing exponentially with each attempt.

> **authorization validated. pass user** < the watchdog replied and with that the system opened itself to her. Disgustingly easy, Raven reflected as she streaked through the access node; she could have designed a better security system in her sleep.

Deep inside the government system now, she paused a little and allowed fragments of her consciousness to snake out in all directions, searching according to the parameters she had already set. She relaxed, sinking into a semi-aware state, feeling her sphere of influence extending all around her. Suddenly there was a tweak at the end of one of her tendrils of thought. All the others raced to meet it. It was another access node, leading into a secondary system. Raven could not have explained how, but she knew that what she sought lay beyond that gate. Another watchdog approached. Raven didn't wait for it to question her. Instead she overwhelmed it with a stream of authorizations.

> **open sesame** < The gate swung open at her command.

The new system felt darker, there were more shielded databases, security hung over everything like a fog. But none of this impeded Raven. It took her microseconds to identify the system as that belonging to the Security Services. One more microsecond and it was completely under her command. She hadn't entered this system before and therefore took slightly longer to explore it. She was reassured to find no record of her existence in the database; Wraith was equally invisible to the Seccies. A flicker to the edge of her search parameters informed her that Kez had two convictions for theft. A thought erased the data; Kez became invisible to the system. Then she found it. The contents of a datafile filled her mind. A Security Services team, accompanied by three CPS operatives, took into custody a ten-year-old Hex named Rachel Hollis on the fifteenth of March 2366.

Raven imprinted the contents of the file on her eidetic memory, but did not erase the original from the system. Among the threads of data that accompanied the file was a string of numbers and characters designed to execute a lead away from the government system to an alternative address. Raven dived through the net, information whirling above and beneath her. The location of the system she was heading for was more impressively shielded than anything she'd seen before and her search took her on a roller-coaster ride through the net. Any other hacker would have been shaken off long ago but Raven found it as exhilarating as the flitter ride she had forced Kez to take. She felt the same way about speed as she did about loud music; the more of it the better. Finally she crashed through four secured nodes in a row before coming to rest at the main entrance to the central system of the CPS.

The gates into the system were firmly shut; no

watchdog program waited for her outside. With a mental shrug Raven exerted a little pressure and the security sprang to life with the most advanced question and answer routine she had ever encountered.

> ?who <
> accepted user < she told it.
> ?authorization <
> authorization provided <
> password <
> correct password < Raven was disappointed. It was easier to fool this system than she had anticipated. It was designed to catch out an illegal access attempt by requesting certain responses. But Raven, deep in the heart of the net, need only tell the circuitry that she had provided the correct answers for it to believe her. In another few microseconds she had gone through an elaborate sequence of security protocols none of which put up the slightest resistance at all. Finally the system delivered itself up to her just as absolutely as the government system had.

> **you may enter. database records/programs/ operating specifications of this system are at your disposal.** < If Raven had been present in the flesh she would have laughed. The system of the main agency for exterminating Hexes had just thrown itself open to one of them without providing any resistance at all.

But entering the system did not automatically provide Raven with the answers she needed. It took her a while to find the entries for the date 15.03.2366. And more microseconds passed before she located the entry she wanted. It was three lines long.

> at 1400 hours three CPS operatives (names appended) collected suspected Hex—Rachel Hollis—from her place of residence. at 1530 hours the Hex was delivered to Dr. Kalden. background trace results in database. < Raven called up the database and discovered that the CPS had traced Rachel as far back as her adoption in 2361 by Carl and Vanessa Michaelson in Denver, Colorado, USA. They had even discovered the specific orphan asylum and it was at that point that Raven discovered the single most alarming line of data that had ever drawn her attention.

> ?siblings ?Hexes. initial search = no results. ?indepth search <

For a moment Raven considered erasing the whole entry, the whole database if necessary. She would have been prepared to crash the entire system to protect herself. But a moment's thought assured her that this was unnecessary. Instead she appended an addendum to the file.

> indepth search completed. results negative. no siblings exist. results confirmed. no further investigation possible. < Having achieved what she considered the most important point, concealing her own existence, Raven continued her investigation, centering in on Dr. Kalden.

She discovered something surprising. Raven had never bothered to think much about the CPS. Her priority had been to stay out of the sight of any official databases and out of the way of any security services. Gangers in Denver had considered that hiring Raven was worth the trouble of putting up with her difficult personality because she was so meticulous in keeping them out of the sight of the law. But now that Raven was actually inside the system of an agency devoted to exterminating Hexes, she found it was not exactly what she might have expected.

The European arm of the Center for Paranormal Studies was run by Governor Charles Alverstead, who was politically responsible only to the central parliament of the European Federation. But underneath him was a whole host of operatives who were responsible for the day-to-day running of the agency. From what Raven could discover they were apparently divided into three main categories. Two of these were what she might have expected. There were the administrators and investigators whose work was to track down suspected Hexes. Then there were the operatives who processed known Hexes to the death chambers where they were given lethal injections to exterminate them. All of this was what Raven had anticipated and she was unaffected by the cold-bloodedness of the operation. What had surprised her was the existence of a third area of the CPS where no other area should have existed. What else was there for an extermination agency to do?

References to this third area were obscure, mentioning only Dr. Kalden and results obtained by his department. Raven had to search through the files for over an hour of real time before she could piece together the fragments of information to get some kind of idea of the overall picture. Her conclusions were staggering.

When the CPS had been converted from a research department to an extermination agency, in the year 2098, it had retained a portion of its original facilities for surgical experimentation—principally a laboratory and hospital where the initial investigations of the Hex gene had taken place. That facility had remained largely disused until over two hundred years later, in 2320, when suddenly all references to it were classified as confidential. Raven deduced that the laboratory had started up again to continue the experiments. Nothing else could explain the information in the databases. The majority of Hexes were listed as collected by operatives and exterminated according to the due process of law. But one in eight had the same entry as Rachel's file, concerning the Hex's delivery to Dr. Kalden. Raven could draw only one conclusion.

Detaching herself from the system Raven raced back through the net, making each connection with the speed of thought. Reaching her own terminal she rejoined her body in an instant and turned round.

"Wraith," she said. "I think Rachel's still alive."

As the leader of a vast corporation Bob Tarrell was used to working fast. It had been Wednesday afternoon when he had his conversation with the Belgravia Complex's new resident. By Thursday morning he had informed the staff of the Mirage vidchannel that he would be changing its entire format. By midday the same day, six different program proposals lay on his desk and the wheels were in motion for announcing the launch of a radical new rock channel that weekend at his party.

Although prior commitments had prevented him from meeting Elizabeth Black at his offices, he had contacted her via her vidcom. The image on his screen had looked tired and overworked but when he told her of his plans for an alternative rock channel she had agreed to download all the information she had on rock music through the net. It had arrived within the hour. The speed had impressed the media magnate and he was seriously considering offering the young researcher a job. He had attempted to call the management of AdAstra as well but their line had been engaged consistently. However, one of his assistants had linked up with their computer database which, although small, had provided the information about channel ratings which he had wanted.

The board of directors had voted unanimously in favor of Bob's proposal to alter Mirage's format and the shareholders, concerned about its consistently dropping ratings, had welcomed the chance to revive its fortunes. Already several well-known presenters had been wooed away from other music channels with the promise of larger salaries and the hope of achieving cult status. Mirage's logo had vanished from holoscreen billboards and the channel's main studios. Already artists had submitted graphic designs for the logo of CultRock.

Personally Bob Tarrell considered 20th-century rock music to be the most horrific din but the initial reactions from his company had confirmed his belief that there was money in it. Therefore he had let it be known that he had a great admiration for the genre. As interest in the new channel grew steadily, Bob

Tarrell had visions of revitalizing the entire music scene.

While her father was pretending an interest in alternative rock music his daughter had made the decision to despise it. This considered judgment had been the result of sitting through three hours of it with Caitlin and Zircarda. All three would have been perfectly willing to hail it as the most exciting thing they had ever heard. But when the final track had eventually screeched to an end, Zircarda, lifting a cautious hand to her ringing ears, had said deliberately:

"I don't think it's really us, do you?"

Sighing with relief, Ali and Caitlin had concurred willingly. Although all three had congratulated Bob Tarrell on his wild idea and assured him that it would be the latest craze, within an hour the word had discreetly been spread to the rest of the clique that CultRock was not for them. Naturally this made no difference to the group's plans to come to Tarrell's glitzfest that weekend. Rubbing shoulders with celebrities was worth pretending an interest in alternative rock for an evening.

In any other situation Raven would have been ready and willing to help Bob Tarrell with the launch of his new channel. But ever since she had discovered the puzzle within the CPS's database she had been hacking through the net in the attempt to gain more information. She had only halted her search twice. Once to speak to Bob Tarrell over the vidcom and send him information on alternative rock music and once to set up a system for the nonexistent company AdAstra, complete with a faulty vidcom line. Interest in Raven's preferred musical genre had been snowballing and the only reason Wraith had not been warning her about unnecessary exposure was that he was so wrapped up in the possibility that Rachel was still alive.

The information she had found about the Hex laboratory was scarce. The only addition to the scraps of data she had already discovered was the issue of the lab's connection to Dr. Kalden. The date when all references to the disused lab became confidential was the same as the date given for Kalden, then twenty-three, leaving a highly lucrative research post. After that all references to him seemed to cease. He stopped publishing in the scientific and medical journals where he had once been an authority on experimental neural psychology. He broke all contact with the remaining members of his family and hadn't registered to vote in forty-seven years.

Raven found this suspicious enough to center her research on Kalden. But her probing of the net yielded nothing more concrete. The last picture of Kalden showed him as a young man whereas now he must be seventy years old. It showed an anonymous scientist, dressed plainly in white, the only distinguishing mark a pair of piercing blue eyes. In or out of the net Kalden was a shadow. Anyone but Raven might have believed him dead. But the datapaths only she could trace, the information hidden to any other eyes, and her own instinct convinced her he was still alive. As she stared at the scientist's unreadable eyes she was certain there would be some way to find out where he was.

Many miles away Luciel stared into the same pair of cold blue eyes. He was still weak from the ravages of the last drugs to pass through his body but he tried to keep upright as the scientists examined him. There was no way to conceal his weakness from them but he was scared to collapse in front of Kalden. The doctor rarely participated in the experimentation, although he devised most of it. The only reasons for him to attend a session were if a subject was yielding especially rewarding results or was providing particularly useless data. In the latter case his presence would mean Luciel was scheduled for extermination since no more use could be made of him.

Luciel couldn't believe Kalden could be there because the experiments had shown anything positive. Day after day he was pumped full of drugs and wired up to machinery he couldn't begin to understand. Scanners measured electrical impulses in his brain and the machinery but he couldn't imagine what the scientists could be learning from him. They went through the motions of the experiments with mechanical precision but they seemed uninterested in the findings. Luciel suspected he rarely provided them with any usable results. Half the experiments they performed seemed futile and some seemed to have no reason other than to break his spirit.

As well as the bruises from the injections, his skin was covered in faded scars and burns. His dreams when delirious were nightmares, but even through the clouds of hallucination he knew that some of what he remembered was true. The metal chair they strapped him in, the electric current that raced through his body a hundred times as fast as the flutters of his beating heart and the smell of his own skin burning when the power was turned up too high. These were things he believed in and when Kalden fixed him with that considering stare Luciel felt as frightened as a laboratory rat with as little hope of saving himself.

Raven had been unable to prove her suppositions. Theoretically if a laboratory was performing secret experiments on Hexes, a computer database of their results should exist. But Raven could find no system that corresponded to that of the laboratory. She searched consistently for two whole days before finally detaching herself from the terminal and smashing her fist against the keypad with frustration.

"Nothing!" she seethed. "I swear, if there was anything there I'd have found it by now."

"Maybe your hypothesis was incorrect," Wraith said and Kez flashed him a warning look. But Raven seemed too angry with the terminal to care.

"I'm not wrong," she told him. "The laboratory exists. I could even make a guess as to where it is. But I can't find the computer system." She massaged the back of her neck, her movements heavy with exhaustion.

"Maybe you should get some sleep," Kez suggested cautiously.

"Not until I've worked this out," Raven replied firmly. Crossing over to the Nutromac she ordered tea and carried the cup over to the couch, sitting beside Wraith and stretching her legs out in front of her. Kez sat opposite, watching as she sank into the cushions.

"Perhaps the CPS hid the system so that it couldn't be found by a Hex," Kez said.

"That's what I would have thought," Raven replied. "But you haven't seen their main system. It was pitifully easy to hack into. Even a regular hacker could have cracked it in time."

There was a pause. Raven had closed her eyes and was beginning to drift off into sleep before Wraith suddenly spoke.

"Raven," he said, frowning.

"What?" She opened one eye, apparently wondering if it was worth her while to listen to him.

"Do the CPS know that you're more than just a regular hacker?" he asked.

"The CPS don't even know I exist," Raven replied. "And I intend to keep it that way."

"You're missing the point," Wraith shook his head. "What I meant was, do they know what any Hex can do?"

"Explain," Raven said, both eyes open now.

"I've never known another Hex apart from you," Wraith told her, "so I don't know if this is right. But all of your mutant abilities are connected to computers, are they not?"

"More or less," Raven sat up. "There are other aspects, but the basic bent is clearly technological."

"Does the CPS know that?"

"I don't know," Raven frowned. "At least, I'm not certain, because I haven't found the results of any recent experiments." Then she shook her head. "No, Wraith, you're wrong. They must know, that's how the Hex gene was created in the first place."

"How?" Kez asked. He hadn't really expected Raven to answer but she turned to look at him with a sudden interest.

"Kez, what do you know about Hexes?" she asked. "I mean, what did you know before you met me?"

"I figured it was like magic," he said slowly, a little embarrassed. "Or aliens, something like that. I had no idea it involved computers."

Raven nodded slowly, glancing at Wraith who was watching her intently. Then she began to speak, thinking out loud.

"Most people don't know anything about Hexes, except that they're illegal," she said. "The genetics experiments and the extermination laws are ancient history now."

"That was when the Hex gene was created?" Wraith asked.

"Don't you know any history either?" Raven raised her eyebrows.

"Gangers generally have their minds on other things," Wraith pointed out dryly.

"OK," Raven shrugged. "There's not much to tell." She looked at Kez. "But it's connected to what I was telling you the other day about the rush to create more advanced technology during the 21st century. One of the areas that was affected was genetic research. A lot of mutated genes were grafted on to human DNA. They were designed to make the human race more efficient and adaptable. Most of the mutations didn't have much effect so in the end the experimentation was abandoned. But the Hex gene which was created was widely adopted until 2098 when Hexes were made illegal."

"Why was it widely adopted?" Wraith asked.

"It was designed to increase computer literacy," Raven told him. "They were trying to improve programming skills, things like that."

"So, why are Hexes exterminated?" Kez asked. "I would have thought that computer literacy was a good thing."

"Something must have gone wrong," Wraith mused.

"The extermination laws were passed in 2098," Raven said.

"And you don't know why?" Kez asked.

"The whole thing was shrouded in secrecy," Raven told him. "Sanctioning the murder of a whole sub-strain of mutated humans is a controversial thing to do."

"Do you think they found out about what you can do?" Kez asked.

"They must have guessed that a Hex could become the ultimate hacker," Raven said. "But I'm more than just a hacker—nothing I've found in the CPS's system indicates that they know about the way I enter the net."

"Raven, an intelligent hacker would be bad enough," Wraith said. "Computers are used all over the world. International government and finance depends on those systems being secure."

"So they started exterminating," Raven agreed. "Maybe before they had the chance to work out exactly how far the Hex abilities extend. That would explain why they reopened that lab—to investigate what we can actually do." Then she slammed a hand onto the arm of the couch. "But none of this is helping me find that system."

"If it exists, it's meant to be secret," Wraith pointed out. "Experimenting on humans is illegal, even Hexes."

"Raven, how would *you* set up a secret system?" Kez asked shyly. Raven grinned at his admiring tone of voice, then narrowed her eyes as she thought.

"I'd keep it independent of the net," she said slowly. "Accessible through only one terminal."

"Can that be done?" Wraith asked.

"Perhaps," Raven nodded. "But if that's what the laboratory is using we won't find out if Rachel is still alive without breaking into it."

Ali studied herself in the full-length mirror. The holodress shimmered when she moved, projecting images of a flurry of rainbow crystals circling her figure. She smiled at her reflection, while the mirror doubled the swirl of phantom crystals, then swayed out of the way to avoid being squashed by Caitlin. They were in Zircarda's parents' apartment. All Saturday afternoon people had been arriving at the Tarrell apartment to set up for the party, and all afternoon the three girls had been dressing up. Caitlin's glossy curls now betrayed a new hint of auburn, which contrasted vividly with her forest-green dress, made from individual leaves spun together and preserved by an artificial gelling agent. Zircarda was wearing red. Her fascination with ganger-style fashion had made her spend a huge amount of money on a genuine real leather dress in a signal-flare crimson. Now she stepped in front of Caitlin to check her makeup. Ali sat back on the bed as Zircarda looked flirtatiously at her reflection through long eyelashes. Caitlin joined her and smiled conspiratorially.

"I can't wait to meet your Dad's guests," she whispered. "There was an item on the news today about the launch of CultRock."

"I know, I saw it," Ali grimaced. "I just hope they won't be playing that kind of music all evening."

"Maybe we should get a move on," Caitlin suggested. "It's nearly eight."

"What time were people supposed to arrive, Ali?" Zircarda asked casually.

"Start time's seven thirty," Ali told her.

"It's still a little early," Zircarda frowned.

"It doesn't really matter, though," Ali reminded her. "I'm almost the hostess, aren't I? So I can be as early as I want."

"OK, then." Zircarda reached for her coat. "I'll call a flitter."

"We could walk, and be there before the flitter arrives," Caitlin pointed out.

"I think we should take a flitter," Zircarda said firmly and the other two shrugged and agreed.

*   *   *

When they eventually got there, Ali hardly recognized her own apartment. Rock music pounded out of huge speakers and the four main rooms were packed solid with celebrities. Even Zircarda was a little intimidated. Instead of trying to approach someone like Yannis Kastell or Elohim, two of the most popular artists of the day, she clustered with the rest of the clique in the corner of the room sipping champagne and pointing out celebrities to each other.

Just as Ali wondered if she would be spending the entire evening as a wallflower, her father caught sight of her and waved. Smiling, Ali went to greet him, followed closely by Zircarda. Bob slung an arm around his daughter's shoulders and ruffled her hair.

"This is my daughter Ali," he said to the man he had been talking to. "Ali, this is Gideon Ash. He'll be hosting a program on the new channel."

"Pleased to meet you, Mr. Ash," Ali said politely, shaking hands with the presenter, before a movement beside her reminded her to introduce him to Zircarda. Listening to a somewhat desultory conversation about the new channel, the two girls were ideally positioned to catch the first glimpse of Bob Tarrell's star guest, as she entered the apartment.

"Elizabeth!" he called and, forging a path through the other guests, went to greet her, followed by Gideon Ash, Zircarda and Ali. "I thought you were never coming!"

A glance sideways told Ali that Zircarda's face had the same frozen look she could feel on her own. She had an instinctive feeling that she wasn't going to like Elizabeth Black. The girl looked younger than

she did but she had an utter possession that made
Zircarda's self-confidence seem weak in comparison.
She wore a skin-tight black catsuit that displayed to
advantage a perfect figure, covered by a loose mesh
tunic of platinum chain-links. A cloud of black hair
framed her face and her black eyes were outlined in
gold. It was several moments before Ali even noticed
her two companions. Kez, dressed simply in dark
red and a tall man with perfect features, dead white
skin, and starkly white hair, dressed entirely in black
cycle leathers. Elizabeth stepped forward and took
Bob Tarrell's outstretched hand, supremely unconscious that people were turning to look at her.

"How are you, Bob?" she smiled. "This is my
cousin, Kez, and my friend, Ryan. Ryan's a holovid
producer."

"I'm pleased to meet you," Bob told them both,
shaking hands earnestly. "And, Elizabeth, you look
incredible tonight. Truly electric, as my daughter
would say." He motioned Gideon forward. "This is
Gideon Ash, one of my presenters." He paused to
allow Ash to offer an admiring greeting. "Zircarda
Anthony, one of my daughter's friends, and my
daughter herself, Ali. Ali, this is Elizabeth."

"I'm fascinated to meet you, Ali," the black-haired
girl told her, looking directly at her with the darkest
eyes the girl had ever seen.

Ali froze. She couldn't have explained the fear
that had consumed her. But as the young researcher's eyes had met hers the thought had leaped
into the forefront of her mind. *She knows!* It was in-
escapable. Those obsidian eyes had looked straight

through her, had seen her soul. Now Elizabeth was laughing in response to something Bob had said. In another few moments she had moved on to the dance floor, joined in seconds by Elohim, who was wasting no time in introducing himself. It wasn't until Zircarda had been speaking for some time that Ali connected with reality again.

"Can you believe that outfit?" her friend was asking with a barely concealed jealousy.

"What about the way Elohim's all over her?" a voice chimed in from behind and Ali didn't need to look to know that it belonged to Caitlin. "She's younger than us, for God's sake!"

Ali wasn't listening. She was frantically studying Elizabeth's two companions. Kez was looking around him with a bemused fascination, but the white-haired man was leaning against the wall. His eyes, covered with dark shades, could be watching anyone. Ali shuddered. She was wondering wildly if they could possibly be from the CPS despite the fact that the logical part of her brain was telling her that the CPS would hardly bother to engage in such a pointless masquerade.

Raven was high on celebrity. For the first time since arriving in London she was actually enjoying herself. Wraith had been conducting his search for Rachel with a single-minded monotony that came close to driving her insane with boredom. But recent events, moving into the Belgravia Complex, the mystery of the secret laboratory and the launch of CultRock were bringing Raven back to life. She felt the pounding music flood through her, echoing the beat of her heart, in the darkened room and grinned fiercely.

It had been a surprise to see Ali. She might have made the connection between Bob Tarrell and the stranger in the network earlier if she hadn't been sluggish with boredom. The moment of recognition hadn't actually come until Bob had introduced his daughter. The fear that had leaped into the girl's eyes as Raven had studied her had confirmed it. Raven was amused at the incongruity. If she hadn't known for a fact that the spoiled, shallow socialite was a Hex she would never have believed it.

If Wraith had known Ali's secret he would probably have demanded that Raven show her how to avert her danger. Raven dismissed the idea with contempt. The only sure way for a Hex to escape the eagle eyes of the CPS was to become invisible, to fade out of the world as she had done. The girl suppressed a laugh, thinking how successful her own fade had been, enough so that she could be standing in the middle of a room of celebrities, and yet, she might as well have not been there. Being here at all was a risk, but Raven enjoyed the danger. Ali didn't look as if she was enjoying it. A glance to the side of the room gave Raven a split-second glimpse of Ali's tense expression. This time she did laugh aloud. What use would it do for her to warn Ali to run? There was no way a spoiled little rich girl would survive out in the real world.

Bob Tarrell announced the launch of CultRock at midnight. His guests, high on vintage champagne, cheered enthusiastically. A generous man by nature, Bob gave full credit for the inspiration to Elizabeth Black, a researcher from AdAstra, and the girl returned his compliments politely. Everything was exactly as might have been expected. But Ali, separated from her celebrity-spotting friends, felt as if she had been turned to stone. She couldn't even lift her glass in the obligatory toast. When she finally lifted the champagne to her lips with a leaden hand, she might have been drinking stale water for all the enjoyment she got from it.

It was like the worst kind of nightmare. All her senses were screaming danger, and there was nothing she could do about it. Dark eyes regarded her from across the room, then flickered away as if the glance had only been accidental. Ali knew better. That casual smile was as treacherous as the grin of a crocodile.

It wasn't until the early hours of the morning, when the guests finally departed and Ali curled up in a ball under the white counterpane of her bed, that the fear finally began to recede. But her dreams that night were menacing and confused, running from something she couldn't see with legs that refused to bear her weight. The appearance of the girl had been a catalyst. She had brought to life all the anxiety that Ali had tried to suppress since the discovery of her own deadly secret. For the first time in her life, Ali Tarrell was possessed by terror.

5

Light Thickens

Three sets of architectural blueprints from different elevations were spread out on the floor of the lounge. Raven, back in her rumpled army cast-offs, her hair once more a wild mass of tangles, sat cross-legged in front of them, holding a stylus. Wraith sat across from her, studying them equally intently, and Kez, kneeling on the couch, leaned over the back, looking down on them.

Raven's brows were drawn into a frown and Kez was not surprised when, throwing down the stylus, she shook her head.

"It's not going to work this way, Wraith."

"It's all we have to go on," Wraith replied, not looking up from the plans.

"Wraith," Raven said, waiting until she had got his full attention. When his eyes finally met hers she went on. "These are the design blueprints for the original laboratory—they were all I could pull out of the CPS database. By now that entire facility will have been remodeled." She stood up, and crossed to the couch. "These plans are about three hundred years old."

"Do you have any other suggestions?" Wraith asked.

"I will have."

"That's not good enough," he told her. "We've got to get into that lab as soon as possible."

"Well, why don't you ask Kez for an idea?" Raven suggested nastily. "I don't recall that he's been that much use so far."

"We didn't bring Kez to help us find Rachel," Wraith said with exasperation. "He's here because you brought him with us on a whim."

"And I can easily hit the road if you've changed your mind," Kez told her, angry and disenchanted with Raven.

Raven was smiling; she was bored and frustrated, and baiting Wraith and Kez was the only thing she could do to remove her apathy, other than turning on the sound system to its highest volume, or taking off in the flitter and hot-wiring the acceleration. But it didn't take Raven long to switch from boredom to anger and Kez's next comment provided the necessary spark.

"Maybe I do have an idea," he told her. "If you're so keen to get into that lab why don't you turn yourself over to the CPS?"

"What a sensational idea," she hissed at him. "Why don't you make the call and see what I do to you."

"Hey, Raven, stay chill," Kez said uneasily, and Wraith came to his rescue. Finally standing up and abandoning the plans he walked round to stand behind Kez, resting a light hand on his shoulder.

"It's not actually a bad idea," he said calmly. "Why shouldn't we try it, Raven?"

"It would be me trying it, not you," she told him. "And there's no chance."

"If you can get in and out of the CPS's database as easily as you claim, surely you can get in and out of the laboratory?"

"They wouldn't take me to the laboratory," Raven said unequivocally. "I've been working out how they decide who to take to the lab." She locked eyes with Wraith, trying to convince him. "It wouldn't be me."

"Why not?" Kez asked and Wraith added:

"I'm not sure I believe you, Raven."

"Sit down," Raven commanded, waiting until Wraith had complied, seating himself on the arm of the couch. He hadn't dropped his eyes and she smiled slightly at the intensity of his scrutiny.

"Go on, then," he said. "Convince me."

"Did I tell you the CPS take one in eight of the suspected Hexes they capture to the laboratory?" Raven asked. Wraith gave a brief nod and she continued: "There's a pattern to that. They always take the youngest and most inexperienced. The ones that are found through medical results or unusual behavior, not the convicted computer hackers, and never anyone older than about twenty. It's almost always children, as well."

"You're only fifteen, Raven," Wraith pointed out.

"And for all your illegal ventures into the net, it's not as if you've ever been discovered. You fit into those categories."

"No I don't," she shook her head. "I may be barely an adult as far as the CPS and you are concerned, but I've been active as a Hex for a long time. I don't think I've reached the height of my abilities, but they certainly extend far further than those of the novices the CPS like to experiment on. I'm much too dangerous to them. They'd work that out in five minutes; even they can't be that stupid. And then they'd exterminate me, without even waiting for an official authorization."

"I thought you always said there was no way the CPS could do that to you," Kez pointed out.

"That's because they would *never* get me as far as one of their facilities," she informed him coldly. "If the CPS did ever arrive to collect me, which I doubt would happen because I've taken precautions against it, they wouldn't get me more than ten meters. Their vehicles would shut down, their communicators wouldn't work and either I'd escape or they'd kill me." She shrugged. "It's as simple as that. And it's not a risk I'd be willing to take for *anyone*."

"I suppose I can't blame you," Wraith said slowly. "And, in this case, I do believe you."

"Thank you," Raven replied with exaggerated sarcasm.

"But we've still got to find a way into that facility," Wraith added. "Even if we can't use you as bait."

* * *

Ali was in her room when it happened. She was lying on her bed, feeling particularly bedraggled. Zircarda and Caitlin were still recovering from the excesses of the night before and Ali, even though she'd barely drunk anything, felt as if she had all the after-effects. She lay on her stomach, staring across the room at the blank screen of her computer terminal. She hadn't used it in nearly a week.

The last time she had attempted to do so she had found herself slipping into the trance that had overtaken her once before while working at the terminal. Ali sighed. That first time had been almost wonderful, certainly the most exciting thing that had ever happened to her, and when she had realized what it had signified she had almost been pleased. Being a Hex seemed somehow special. It was not until the second time she had tried it that she had been scared. She shivered, remembering how it had felt to be caught and held against her will. Then the sudden outward flood of information that had overwhelmed her, the stranger's contempt coupled with the conviction that Ali would be caught and exterminated. That other essence had read her mind in a split second, but given nothing away itself.

The simple fact that someone existed who knew her secret had terrified Ali. Then, yesterday, she had met someone else who knew it, who had looked through her and with a glance turned her inside out. Ali buried her head in her arms, wishing with all her might that Elizabeth Black would go back to America, and even more fervently that the Hex gene had never even existed.

A faint noise, just on the edge of hearing, made her look up again, frowning. She listened intently, hearing nothing. But it had been a sound that she knew. Instinctively she glanced over at the terminal and suddenly knew what had caught her attention. It had been the sound of the computer powering up. She watched it with fixation, as if the sleek gray wall unit was a deadly snake. The screen was glowing, showing that it was on. But it was impossible for the terminal to switch itself on.

Then slowly, inexorably, letters began to march across the screen. Too far away for Ali to read them, but unmistakably letters. And yet no one had touched the keypad, none of this was possible. The letters came to a halt; a single sentence now glowed on the screen. The room suddenly seemed much colder and very dark. Ali crossed to the terminal, moving as if she was made of glass and a sudden movement might break her. The sentence faced her, starkly uncompromising.

> come to apartment 103 immediately <

It was almost innocent. A simple request. But it had appeared almost supernaturally on the screen. And it was not a request. It was a demand. One that Ali did not dare refuse.

She picked up her synthetic woolen jacket and put it on, then she walked toward the door, like someone approaching their execution. She didn't even notice the terminal switching itself off behind her. She left the apartment with leaden footsteps, the door swishing shut behind her. Slowly she walked along the covered security-shielded walkways that would take her to her destination. She reached it in less than fifteen minutes. The outer door was identical to her own. Reaching out a heavy hand she touched the wall-plate. Three seconds later the door slid open. Someone had been waiting for her. Ali took a deep breath and stepped inside. Behind her the door slid shut again.

Raven smiled icily as the teenager entered the apartment. She was not happy about the course of action she had chosen. She didn't like revealing herself in this way, but betraying some of her Hex abilities had been necessary to intimidate Ali. She might have managed to maintain her disguise for a short while at Tarrell's glitzfest, but she had no expectation of sustaining that image without an added lever. Looking at the slim blonde girl, facing her across the room, Raven was conscious of feeling annoyed. Ali was slightly taller than her.

Raven had never felt inferior to anyone. At nine years old she had forced people to respect her in order to survive. Her ability to do things far beyond the capabilities of other people meant that most of the time she considered herself superior to anyone else. As a person and as a Hex, Ali was beneath her contempt. But Ali was the spoiled daughter of a wealthy and influential man; Kez had told her all about the Gateshall clique before their visit to the Tarrells' apartment. For an instant, as Ali entered the room, Raven felt like a streetrat from the slums of Denver, and she had to force her hands not to curl into fists.

Ali's eyes were wide with apprehension as she

looked at the younger girl. The sophisticated Elizabeth Black, whom Zircarda had been so jealous of, had melted away. In her place, dressed in black army gear, staring straight at her, was the stranger in the matrix. The veneer of deceptive artifice had cracked, revealing something rawer and much more dangerous. For the first time in her life Ali faced someone who had the power to destroy her and the will to do it. But strangely, she didn't shudder. She had passed beyond terror and her voice was level as she spoke.

"Who are you?"

Dark eyes flashed, something unpleasant glinting in their depths. But for once, their owner did not even consider dissembling.

"Call me Raven."

"What do you want?" Ali held herself perfectly still, awaiting the answer. Before Raven could reply, the door opened.

Wraith and Kez stopped dead as they saw Ali. Raven hadn't expected them to be back so quickly. Now she resigned herself to the inevitable, as Wraith placed the two heavy duffel bags he was carrying on the floor, and turned to confront her.

"Raven?" he asked.

"Come in, Wraith," she told him. "Both of you, you might as well hear this as well."

"Hear what?" Kez asked, studying Ali curiously.

"Sit down," Raven insisted, including Ali in the invitation, and seating herself where she could keep her eyes on the girl. "I think I might have found us a way into that lab."

Kez's eyes widened incredulously, but Wraith was

quicker to comprehend. He looked seriously at Ali who was sitting uneasily on the edge of a chair, before looking back at Raven.

"Does she know?" he asked.

"Do I know what?" Ali demanded. Now that she didn't have to face Raven alone she was becoming bolder and Raven realized it. In a moment she had seized the initiative again.

"I was just about to explain it to her," she told Wraith. Then she fixed Ali with a level stare. "How long have you known you were a Hex?" she asked.

"Me?" Ali froze to her seat, but it was no more than she had expected, and she answered honestly, fixed in the headlight glare from Raven's eyes. "Only about a month." She hesitated. "Are you going to turn me in?"

"No," Wraith replied, unequivocally, earning himself a disapproving sideways glance from Raven.

"You're a Hex too, aren't you?" Ali said. "It was you I met in the network that time."

"Yes, it was me." Raven leaned back in her chair. "And I'm not going to turn you in, although everything I warned you about still holds true. I'm going to offer you a proposition. And you would be wise to accept it."

"What kind of proposition?" Ali asked suspiciously. Strangely enough, the dark-eyed girl was beginning to remind her of Zircarda; she had the same look in her eyes that the leader of the Gateshall clique got when she was determined to do something.

"Let me explain," Wraith intervened. "It's a long story."

"Go on," Ali waited.

"None of us are exactly what we seem to be,"

Wraith began and Ali raised her eyebrows expectantly, hardly surprised. He smiled wryly and continued: "Raven and I are brother and sister. We, and Kez," he glanced briefly at the boy, "have been searching for my other sister, Rachel . . ."

As Wraith elaborated, Ali slowly began to relax. The story was one of the strangest she had ever heard, involving gangers, government organizations, secret laboratories and covert plans. It was almost as implausible as a vidfilm, but somehow Ali believed it. The strangest part of all was Wraith's account of how they gained their information. Ali was fascinated by the idea of how Raven was able to control the network, but the younger girl volunteered no information and Ali was too intimidated by her stark stare to ask any questions. But Wraith's measured explanation, coupled with the fact that it didn't look as if she was going to be turned over to the CPS, was gradually calming her down. But when Wraith reached his conclusion her alarm returned.

"You want to use me as bait for the CPS?" she said in shock.

"It's our best chance of finding Rachel," Wraith began but Ali didn't let him finish.

"No chance," she told him, standing up to leave. "I'm not doing this." She shook her head. "I'm sorry, Wraith. But I doubt your sister's even alive. The CPS kill people, and I don't want to be one of them."

"Don't be so hasty," Raven snapped. "You might regret it."

"Are you threatening me?" Ali asked, and Raven smiled.

"No," Wraith said quietly. "If you're unwilling to

help us, we won't force you. But please give it more consideration."

"I can't," Ali told him. "I'm sorry." With that, she turned and left the apartment without looking back.

Wraith watched her go with troubled gray eyes, but he didn't try to stop her. As the door swished shut behind Ali, Raven hissed with annoyance.

"I could have made her do it," she told him.

"She's only a child, Raven," he said sternly. "I refuse to allow you to manipulate her. This is our problem, not hers." For a moment he looked as if he might say something more, but he changed his mind and left the room without adding anything.

Raven and Kez looked at each other. Outmaneuvered, Raven didn't seem to know what to say, and Kez didn't feel in a mood to say anything. Wraith had been scrupulously honest in telling his story to Ali—*too* honest, Kez felt. The ganger hadn't neglected to mention how Kez had joined their group and he hadn't missed the expression of contempt that crossed Ali's face.

"So much for your idea," he said eventually.

"It was your idea to start off with," Raven reminded him. "I simply provided an alternative Hex."

"Do you know anyone else we could use?" Kez asked.

"What do you think I am?" Raven frowned. "A detective agency? I only found her out by accident when she was fooling around in the net." She drummed her fingers on the side of her chair with irritation.

"You don't like her very much, huh?" Kez asked.

"She's almost as brainless as she looks," Raven

said. Then she gave him a considering look. "Somehow I doubt you'll be seeing much more of that clique she belongs to."

"I don't want to," Kez said angrily. But he was angry with Wraith, rather than Raven. "Let's get out of here," he said impulsively. "Your cover's been blown now, anyway."

"You're right," Raven agreed. "I'm sick and tired of this whole business. If Wraith doesn't like my ideas that's his problem."

"Are you going to give up?" Kez asked.

"Why not?" Raven shrugged. "Anything's got to be more interesting than this."

Kez hesitated. He was angry with Wraith, and Raven's disenchantment with his way of operating was infectious. But he couldn't help remembering how Wraith had looked when he had thought Rachel was dead and, now that he had got involved with the ganger's search, Kez felt reluctant to abandon it so easily. Raven was waiting for him to reply and Kez wanted to be able to agree and just take off with her, despite the fact that he didn't trust her anymore. But he couldn't do it.

"I think we should stick with Wraith," he said reluctantly.

"Wraith can't be helped," Raven told him scornfully. "He's obsessed with ethics—it's like a disease."

"Do you think we could persuade Ali to agree to help us?"

"I could," she shrugged. "But it's no use if Wraith negates everything I say."

"Then we'll have to go around him," Kez told her.

"Oh?" Raven waited curiously, and taking a deep breath, Kez made his suggestion:

"Tell Ali the CPS are already after her," he said. "Then she'd have no reason not to join us. With her inside that lab, we could find Rachel and break them both out. Without us, she'd be stuck there forever."

"As long as she lived," Raven interjected. "We'd have to make sure she got sent to the lab. Otherwise she's no use to us."

"You seemed pretty sure she would be," Kez reminded her.

"I still am," Raven said. "But there's an element of chance in everything." She thought for a moment, then nodded decisively. "We'll do it. But not yet. I have to make the discovery accidentally."

"Why?" Kez looked suspicious and Raven sighed with annoyance.

"Because Wraith has to be the one to tell her," she informed him. "You saw the way she behaved. She trusts him, and she'll believe whatever he tells her."

"That means we've got to convince Wraith too," Kez said doubtfully. Raven shrugged.

"We'd have to do that anyway," she replied. "We couldn't tell Ali something like that without him finding out. But if we can make Wraith believe Ali's in danger and tell her so, she'll do as we say."

"If Wraith finds out we've tricked him . . ." Kez began but Raven interrupted him:

"If he does find out, it'll be too late to object," she declared. "Wraith wants into that lab more than either of us. This is the way to do it."

*　　*　　*

When _____ sted that they move out of the Belgravia _____ x, just in case Ali reported them to the Security Services, Wraith didn't make any objection. He had been against moving into the complex to start off with and, although he didn't think Ali would risk calling out the Seccies, he preferred to err on the side of caution. The next morning, after having been at the complex for less than a week, Elizabeth Black and Kester disappeared. As far as the housing corporation were concerned, they had notified them of their intention not to renew the lease on the apartment for another month, a removal company had been hired to sell the furniture and forward the proceeds to an American bank account, their flitter had been returned to the rental company and Nimbus Airlines' database registered them as having traveled to San Francisco on the 9 a.m. flight, together with a Mr. Ryan Donahue.

In actual fact Wraith, Raven and Kez had moved no further than the Stratos Hotel, signing in under different names and requesting a secluded suite. The hotel had been Raven's choice and she had brought her collection of disks with her, packed into three large crates in the customized skimmer that had replaced the flitter. Apart from that they had mostly traveled light, taking only what they could carry. But this had included the equipment Wraith and Kez had collected.

It was standard electronic equipment, obtainable perfectly legally from any store, but what Raven was using it for was completely unorthodox. Since she had agreed to go ahead with the decision to keep looking for Rachel, even without Ali's assistance, she was making elaborate preparations. Wraith allowed her to make adjustments to his laser pistol, and didn't inquire what she intended to do with the rest of the equipment. He considered himself fortunate that she hadn't flown into a rage after he had stymied her attempts to use Ali as bait. But Kez, who had more or less resolved his difference with Raven, had the heap of electronic innards explained to him in detail during their first day at the hotel.

"Most of this is to do with getting into the lab's system," Raven had explained. "If I can find their central control room I'll be able to control it without physical intervention. But until I get there I'll have to trip circuits and fool security, all of it manually. For that I need tools."

"You're making them yourself?" Kez asked.

"I told you it wasn't just computers I had an affinity with," Raven reminded him. "Who do you think made Wraith's transceiver?" By then Kez had had that device explained to him in more detail than he felt able to cope with, but he knew why Raven had brought up that particular piece of equipment as an example. Among the spaghetti of cables and wires on the long dining table of the hotel suite, was a more delicate piece of electronics. It was tiny, involving micro-circuitry that the stores could not have provided. Raven had produced the miniature circuit-board and some specialized tools from the duffel bag that she had brought with her to gangland when Kez had first met her. From it she had created a transceiver device similar to Wraith's. But this one was not intended to be surgically implanted. It took the form of a plain white ear-stud, something that would hardly be noticed. Especially not when worn by a seventeen-year-old girl. Raven had even produced a matching stud for the other ear, although this one was without circuitry. But the first stud was a piece of equipment any electronics designer would have been proud of. Barely five millimeters in diameter, it contained a transmitter, receiver, location beacon and private sensor. If Kez's plan worked and Ali went into the lab, Raven would be able to keep complete track of her, every second she was there.

Bob Tarrell was surprised by the sudden disappearance of his new acquaintances. But Elizabeth had left a message on his vidcom, apologizing and explaining that AdAstra had unexpectedly recalled her to the States, and after all there was no reason for him to be especially concerned. The media was full of the news of his new channel and the shareholders were predicting a roaring success.

His daughter was more alarmed. She watched the morning news with her father on Monday on Populix, one of his channels. The main story was the launch of CultRock, showing that her father had exploited his ownership of the news channel again. But she was not concentrating on the program. Her thoughts revolved round the gangers' departure and what it signified and she barely noticed the screen until a brief remark at the end of the item.

"While CultRock looks set to be a major success, the U.S. channel that first encouraged this latest music sensa-

tion has gone into receivership. AdAstra is no longer on-line and its database has disappeared from the net." For a split second the reporter's expression wavered between annoyed and puzzled and finally settled on tolerant. *"The channel has refused Populix access to any footage of its programming and has recalled Elizabeth Black, an AdAstra researcher who assisted in the launch of CultRock."* The reporter adopted a more upbeat tone as the channel moved on to show pictures of celebrities arriving at the Tarrells' apartment for the launch of CultRock, and Ali subsided.

Despite the matter-of-fact way the story had appeared on the news, she was suspicious of the official explanation. She knew that Raven wasn't really "Elizabeth Black," and she also had doubts about AdAstra. It seemed a bit too convenient the way the channel had simply disappeared. Obviously the gangers had decided to cover their tracks when they departed. That suited Ali. She hadn't wanted to get involved with them in the first place and the further away they were, the better. She had no intention of reporting them to the Security Services though. Aside from the fact that she was nervous of being questioned about her involvement with them, she had nothing substantial to report. To go to the Seccies with the story she had been told, starring a white-haired ganger called Wraith and his sister, a dangerous and perhaps insane Hex named Raven, would be ludicrous. She kept her own counsel. But it had been difficult for her to cope with the questions of the rest of the clique that day at school.

Listening to the vapid conversation, Ali almost

agreed with Raven's contempt for these people, even though it included her. Her encounter with the gangland Hex had affected her in more ways than she had realized at first, and one of them was the way it had distanced her from the rest of the Gateshall students and her clique in particular. Even though she was safely ensconced in the middle of the group she felt as isolated from them as if the CPS had found her out and were already driving her away. Raven's repeated assertion that she would be caught had sunk in. She was no longer able to convince herself that she was safe. Raven renting that apartment had been like gangers bypassing security and invading the heights of London. Nothing felt normal to Ali anymore.

Kez was feeling equally uncomfortable. He had suggested that they deceive Ali in order to help Wraith. He wanted to help the ganger find his sister and he hadn't forgotten that Wraith had promised to take care of him, while Raven had obviously never even considered it. But, despite wanting to help Wraith, he was beginning to feel that he had made a deal with the devil.

In order to take his mind off how miserable he was, Kez tried to make himself useful. Gradually he was beginning to learn some of the most basic concepts of electronic science, despite the fact that Raven was not the most patient of teachers. Her natural aptitude for anything technological, coupled with her years of experience, made him less than a novice compared to her. But at least he was doing something, and in reward for his persistence Raven didn't subject him to any sudden flares of anger when he made a mistake. He spent most of his time creating the frequency-activated explosive charges with which Raven intended to blast their way into the lab. They were basically simple devices, although Raven supervised the final installment of the charge which would activate the explosive. Wraith obtained more lethal equipment from the Countess and had opened negotiations with her to hire the services of some men to act as muscle back-up when they broke into the facility. The whole operation was looking increasingly serious. Kez doubted that it would succeed the way Wraith envisaged it. But he hoped that, with the additional element that he and Raven were devising, the plan might yet work.

Kez's only worry was how Wraith would react if he discovered what he and Raven had decided to do. He had enough faith in the ganger's perception to suspect that sooner or later Wraith might well find out how Ali had been tricked and he hoped fervently that, if Wraith did find out, it would be too late for him to do anything about it. Otherwise his sense of honor would oblige him to warn her and the operation would be hopeless. Kez knew Raven wouldn't stick with a hopeless cause and he didn't think he could either.

6

Unnatural Troubles

To his surprise, Wraith was becoming interested in politics. The extermination of Hexes, something he had never thought about before in terms of its morality, was troubling him now that Rachel might be one of those at risk. It hadn't affected him so much with Raven. She had always seemed able to take care of herself, and in the slums of Denver, morality was rarely an important consideration. But the Kali's code of honor, that had affected Wraith so much, was making its presence felt.

The people with the Hex gene were the result of a perfectly legal scientific advance. But for over two hundred and fifty years they had been exterminated by their own governments because of the potential threat they posed to the computerized society. Wraith had worked out that even if the CPS only exterminated one person a day, the death count would be nearly a hundred thousand people by now, and

Raven estimated the numbers were far higher. It didn't seem to trouble her that much. Raven had never been particularly interested in other Hexes and was confident enough of her own safety for the massive death tolls to leave her unaffected. But Wraith was more disturbed by them, and especially by the laws that had made this wholesale slaughter legal.

If Hexes had been allowed to exist, Raven would not have had to fear for her life ever since she'd been a child; she might have been a different person without that burden, lacking the manic-depressive streak that made her hell to live with. Ali wouldn't be scared that she would die before she even reached her eighteenth birthday. Rachel wouldn't have been taken away for experimentation at ten years old and delivered to Dr. Kalden's research lab.

The more he considered the whole question of the illegality of Hexes, the more certain Wraith was that the extermination laws were a horrific crime against humanity. But he seemed to be unable to bring Raven and Kez to his way of thinking.

"There's no point in brooding over it," Raven told him, in a bored tone of voice. "I've had to live with this for most of my life. But there's nothing that can be done about it."

"Bad things happen," Kez shrugged. "I was living on the streets at the same age that Raven was fleeing for her life. Gangers have trashed the lower levels of London. People get flatlined every day for no other reason than they were in the wrong place at the wrong time. Little kids get raped and murdered." He shook his head. "You can't *do* anything about it. It's just *there*."

"But it shouldn't be," Wraith insisted, taking hope from the fact that Kez's response had at least showed concern, unlike Raven, who had already turned back to her wires and fuses. "Those things are illegal. But the murder of Hexes is sanctioned by every government in the world. There's nowhere you can escape from the CPS."

"Unless you're good enough," Raven pointed out.

"And how many people are?" Wraith demanded. "You discovered your abilities young enough to be able to use them. Most people are only just working it out when they're hauled off to a death chamber."

"But the government figures that if they weren't, things would be even worse," Kez reminded him. "Raven goes through a computer system like a knife through butter. What if there were thousands of people doing that?"

"Then governments could design better computer systems," Wraith pointed out. "Raven, could you design a system that even you couldn't get into?"

"It's a difficult question," she said thoughtfully. "I would say that the kind of system Dr. Kalden's lab has is one of the best. But if I can physically penetrate the facility, the computers will be a walkover." She thought a while longer. "I might be able to design a system that most Hexes couldn't get into, though," she said eventually. "Maybe even one that it would take me a long time to crack."

"Then why don't the government use Hexes, instead of exterminating them?" Wraith frowned. It was Kez who provided the answer.

"Because it would make people like Raven incredibly powerful," he said. "She could do anything she wanted with the network."

"Most people choose not to act illegally," Wraith said seriously. "Why shouldn't Hexes be the same?"

"I don't think it would work," Kez replied and bent over his own bunch of wires. Wraith fell silent. He could guess what the boy was thinking. Someone like Raven, if there could be more than one of her, wouldn't agree to play by the rules any more than they could be forced to.

They had been at the hotel for two days by the time Raven entered the net again. She told Wraith that she was still unhappy with the scarcity of information on the laboratory and was going to make one last attempt at pulling more information out of the CPS database. Even though her professed intention seemed bland enough, Kez suddenly felt as tense as a spring. This was the moment. He watched Raven disappear into her room with apprehension—she still preferred to keep her ventures into the net private—before bending his head diligently over his work. Wraith asked him a question about how many explosive devices they would have in the end, and he replied mechanically with the figure Raven had determined upon. It seemed to take forever for the girl to finally emerge from her room, although in reality it was only about fifteen minutes.

When she eventually returned to the main room of the hotel suite her eyes were bright with excitement.

"They're after her," she said immediately.

"What?" Wraith looked up and Kez held his breath.

"The CPS," Raven explained. "They're after Ali. They've got a file on her as a suspected Hex."

"Can you remove it from the database?" Wraith asked quickly and mentally Kez kicked himself—he hadn't thought of that. But Raven had obviously anticipated the question.

"It would be counterproductive," she said. "There's certain to be some physical documentation as well. If her file disappeared from the database their suspicions would be confirmed and they'd schedule her for extermination for certain."

Wraith considered for a while, his eyes troubled and his brows furrowed in thought. Finally he came to a decision.

"We have to warn her," he said.

"And get her to help us," Kez put in—after all, Wraith would be surprised if it wasn't suggested. "She hasn't got any choice now."

"Kez is right," Raven agreed. "We're her only way out of the CPS's clutches, just as she's our best shot at getting Rachel out."

"I agree," Wraith nodded. "Can you contact her, Raven?"

"Me?" she grimaced. "Ali wouldn't trust me any further than she could throw me. She'll think I'm just pressuring her. It would be better if you told her, Wraith."

"OK," he agreed. "But we had better not meet Ali here or at the Belgravia Complex. Any suggestions as to a good place to see her?"

"We could pick her up in the skimmer," Raven said.

"But not from the apartment complex," Wraith added. "It's too dangerous."

"Why not from Arkade?" Kez suggested. "They have the most boring collection of junk you've ever seen. No one would notice us picking her up from there."

"The museum?" Raven arched an eyebrow. "Trust you to be original, Kez."

"OK, the museum will do," Wraith agreed. "Raven, send a message to Ali, saying we want to meet with her there this evening at eight."

The skimmer pulled up that evening outside the museum just under one of the glowing streetlamps. Night had fallen on the city, dusk coming early in winter, and all through the levels of London the lights were on. Down in gangland night was dangerous but Arkade had impressive security in order to keep the custom of the families from Belgravia.

Ali stood on the pavement of one of the bridges that enmeshed the recreation complex, waiting for them. Raven, in the driving seat of the skimmer, grimaced slightly as she brought the vehicle to a halt. She was dressed, as always, in black. But her thick silky hair was for once neatly tied back at the nape of her neck in a businesslike way. Kez was sitting in the passenger seat and Wraith waited in the back of the vehicle. As Ali approached, Raven released the security lock on the door, but Wraith had to slide it open himself. Ali got in, closing the door behind her, anxious not to be seen with them and Raven sped the skimmer back into the flow of traffic as Wraith spoke.

"Thank you for agreeing to meet with us," he said.

"I haven't changed my mind, you know," Ali told him. "And you'd better not be planning anything weird." Raven wrinkled her nose and glanced back at the girl, still keeping the skimmer under perfect control. Looking through long lashes she said softly:

"How about a brief trip to gangland, Ali? Do you feel lucky tonight?"

Kez giggled but Wraith looked annoyed.

"Keep us on this level," he warned Raven sharply. "There's no need to play games."

The girl shrugged and turned back to the control console, exchanging an amused glance with Kez who was grinning at Ali's obvious discomfort. But Wraith ignored them.

"Ali," he said. "I'm afraid I have bad news."

"What's happened?" Ali looked alarmed. "Is it to do with your sister?"

"No." Wraith shook his head in reply. "This is about you. It seems the CPS already suspect you of being a Hex."

"Are you sure?" Ali asked, paling. "How do you know? Are they going to come after me ..." Her voice trailed off as her eyes fixed desperately on Wraith, hoping against hope that it was all a mistake. Kez looked studiedly out of the window, unable to look at Wraith and Ali. But Raven's mouth curved in a slow smile.

"Having second thoughts?" she asked softly. Kez

froze and Raven's dark eyes drifted slowly over him before she turned and glanced back at Ali. "About joining us, I mean," she qualified.

"We still won't force you," Wraith added. "But perhaps you should think again."

"It doesn't look like I have much choice, does it?" Ali asked, a little stiffly. But the fact that Wraith had not tried to threaten her made her want to trust him. Her brown eyes narrowed as they met Raven's. The younger girl was apparently taking no notice at all of the controls, but the skimmer sped on smoothly through the evening traffic. "But how do I know you won't just use me to find your sister and then dump me?"

"You don't," Raven replied expressionlessly. But Wraith contradicted her.

"You can trust *me*," he said. "I promise, if you help us, we'll save you from the CPS and help you start a new life somewhere."

If possible Ali turned even paler. Suddenly a new reality was coming home to her. If she was captured by the CPS, even if Wraith managed to rescue her, she could never return to her old life. Belgravia Complex would be the first place the Seccies would look for her, even if her father tried to shelter her from them. And Ali couldn't really believe that Bob Tarrell would give up his media empire, risking imprisonment and disgrace, to hide an illegal mutant from the Security Services, even if the mutant was his daughter. She would truly have nowhere to go without the gangers' help. Her mother was long dead, she had no other close relatives. As for her friends, if the situation had not been so desperate Ali would have laughed. Of all of them Caitlin was the best, but not even Caitlin would suffer the social stigma of even acknowledging a Hex as a friend. She wrapped her arms around herself to keep out the cold. But she didn't permit herself to give in to misery. Raven might have turned back to the skimmer's control panel but Ali could feel her silent gloating. Taking a deep breath the girl looked back at Wraith.

"All right," she said. "I'll join you."

With her father still absorbed in CultRock it was easy for Ali to take a day off school without him noticing. For the last few days he had been leaving early in the morning before Zircarda and Caitlin collected her and not returning until late at night. That Friday, the day after meeting the gangers at Arkade, Ali called Zircarda and told her she was too ill to go into school. After cross-questioning her for ten minutes to make sure that Ali really was sick, Zircarda was apparently satisfied and got off the vidcom. The next call Ali placed was for a flitter to collect her from Belgravia.

In less than half an hour she was entering the suite the gangers had rented at the Stratos, Wraith apparently deciding that it was safe for her to know where they were staying now that she had agreed to help them. The gangers had just finished breakfast and Wraith was piling the remains on a side table to spread out several sheets of design blueprints in front of Ali while Raven finished a cup of black coffee.

As Ali joined them, Wraith reseated himself and

glanced briefly at Raven and Kez, making sure he had their attention, before beginning to speak:

"These are the only plans we have of the laboratory where we believe Rachel is being held," he told her. "Hopefully they'll be good enough to get us into the facility, as most of that will involve just blasting our way in. But we don't have time to mount a long search through the lab, as most of this will be very different by now."

"That's where you come in," Kez said and flushed when she uneasily met his eyes. Wraith didn't appear to notice the tension or if he did, disregarded it.

"We believe that, as a young Hex and somewhat inexperienced, you will probably be automatically taken to this laboratory," he went on.

"I see." Ali had no trouble guessing who had provided that definition of her, but she declined to even look at Raven. "What if they just take me to an extermination facility instead?" she asked.

"The CPS has to get official permission for every extermination," Wraith told her. "You'd be taken to a holding area first, while they sorted out the paperwork. And if that happens we'll abort the plan and get you out straightaway."

"How?" Ali asked.

"We'd hijack the transport on the way from the holding area to the death chambers," Kez told her. "Raven can deal with that, no problem." He looked at the Hex, who was still silently drinking coffee, with an expression that made Ali blink with a sudden realization. She would have laughed. But suddenly Raven looked up and she didn't dare.

"It's most probable that you'll be taken to the laboratory," Wraith was saying. "And, once there, we hope you'll be able to find Rachel for us. I'll show you a holo so you'll know what she looks like."

"What if they keep me in restraints?" Ali asked.

"We hope you'll be mobile for at least part of the time," Wraith told her. "But if anything untoward happens you'll be able to inform us." He looked expectantly at Raven who spoke for the first time.

"You'll be wearing this transceiver," she told Ali, holding out a small object on the palm of her hand. "It took a long time to build it, so don't screw with it, OK?" Her tone was antagonistic and Ali didn't dare do anything more than nod. "Wraith has a similar device surgically implanted," Raven went on. "I can contact him through it, in or out of the network."

"How?" Ali asked in amazement, her surprise getting past her fear of Raven.

"Does it matter?" Raven said sarcastically. "You couldn't do it."

"Are you certain about that?" Wraith asked. "It might be easier if Ali could contact us as well."

"Quite certain," Raven said. "I only gave you your transceiver when we left for Europe, remember? I couldn't have even made it a year before that, let alone even used it. If Ali was capable of that kind of thing, she'd be headed straight for extermination now."

"But could she be?" Kez asked.

"Hypothetically?" Wraith added and Raven sighed.

"If all Hexes have the innate capacity to improve

their skills, then yes," she agreed. "But if there are different levels of ability, it's highly probable that I just have more abilities than Ali." She ignored the older girl's annoyed expression and continued: "I'd like to see what kind of conclusions Dr. Kalden has reached about Hexes. That information should be easy to find when I get into the lab's main database."

"That's what we're planning to do," Wraith informed Ali. "When you've located Rachel, we'll blast our way in. Then Raven will find the lab's control room and enter their computer system. That'll give us control of their security systems and we should be able to get out again without too much trouble."

"Do you want me to find the control room as well?" Ali asked, striving to be as businesslike as Wraith.

"You wouldn't be able to," Raven said briefly.

"There's no real need," Wraith said, less harshly. "The first terminal we find should be able to lead Raven right to it." He hesitated, then added: "And I think Raven's right. You'll be a prisoner there, Ali. I don't think they'll give you a chance to see the control room."

By the time Wraith had explained everything to his satisfaction Ali was feeling exhausted. But the fact that the ganger had turned out to be such a meticulous and conscientious organizer had given her a new confidence in his plan. She could even find herself believing for the first time that everything would be all right. She would find Rachel and then Wraith would come and break them out of the lab. The fact that what would happen after that was still unclear was something Ali didn't allow herself to dwell on.

To her surprise she found herself admiring the ghost-like ganger. Despite his strange white hair he was actually strikingly attractive and had a confidence that made him the accepted leader of the group. Ali tried to ignore the fact that the features that she admired in Wraith were doubled in Raven. She was just as attractive—she had proved that at Ali's father's party even if at the moment she was dressed like a mercenary soldier—and she was the most supremely self-confident person Ali had ever met.

Raven's arrogance was emphasized by the fact that she claimed the CPS had made a mistake in capturing Rachel and that the girl wasn't a Hex at all. Ali couldn't see how it mattered, seeing as Rachel *had* been captured, but Raven obviously took the suggestion that she might have made a mistake as a personal slight.

"I'm willing to bet over half the people they've slaughtered over the years haven't been Hexes either," she insisted. "Just people unlucky enough to be suspected, and then exterminated just in case the suspicions were correct."

"The government wouldn't allow that," Ali said firmly, having gradually gained enough confidence to contradict Raven. "The CPS has to have a warrant for every person they . . . dispose of."

"Dispose of?" Wraith asked. "That's a very callous way of describing it."

"It's legal," Ali said defensively. "You can't deny that."

"I guess you think the government is infallible," Kez interjected. "The Seccies are always happy enough to shoot first and ask questions later—why shouldn't the CPS be the same?"

"It's different in gangland," Ali said coldly. "The Security Services aren't like that up here."

"And you're all law-abiding citizens?" Kez said. "Give it a rest." Wraith looked as if he was about to warn the boy off, but Raven suddenly agreed:

"There isn't so much crime up here, at least not violent crime, but anyone can be guilty of being a Hex. A lot of people the CPS pick up come from families in the heights. Most of them, actually, probably because in gangland people have the sense to run."

"That's how they caught Rachel," Wraith added. "I should have never let that adoption go through."

"Come on, Wraith," Raven said. "You were hardly able to take care of a five-year-old kid. What were you going to do, blast your way through Denver with a little girl holding your hand?"

"You weren't running with a gang," Wraith said, a little harshly.

"I was just a kid myself, Wraith." Raven looked disgusted, too contemptuous of her brother's remark to be angry. "What was I supposed to do? I spent a year living in a cellar before I persuaded people to take me seriously as a hacker." Remembering what company she was in, she turned to look at Ali. "You can sneer at Kez, because you've never had to live on the streets. But if it wasn't for us, who grew up there, you'd have no way to escape the CPS."

"You were just lucky," Ali replied uneasily.

"It wasn't luck," Wraith said, "and Raven's right. But Ali shouldn't have to flee for her life," he added. "Sometimes I doubt I'll ever get this across to you."

"Wraith seems to want to form a solidarity group for Hexes," Raven said, not quite to Ali but in her general direction. "But the fact is that anyone good enough to escape the CPS isn't going to want to load themselves down with people who aren't."

"Then why are you trying to help Rachel?" Ali demanded, taking Raven's remark personally. "Do you care about her or is it just that you think the CPS got it wrong and you're curious to find out why they thought she was a Hex?"

Wraith and Kez exchanged glances—apparently Ali's thoughts had mirrored theirs. But Raven seemed unaffected by their suspicion.

"I don't have to explain myself to you," she said coldly. "Why don't you just concentrate on the fact that I'm going to be saving your life?"

Kez was relieved when Ali finally left in the early afternoon. She had at least stopped looking at him as if he was a bug in her food. It seemed that some of Raven's comments about her privileged lifestyle had struck home. But he still felt uncomfortable with her, and that discomfort was compounded by the fact that it was he who had suggested Raven lie about the CPS being after her.

Ali and Wraith both believed in the lie completely, and Raven seemed utterly unconscious of guilt, now that she had got her own way. She had even given Ali the transceiver with relatively good humor, although she had insisted that the girl did not remove it at all. Ali was sufficiently scared of the CPS to obey Raven, despite her clear dislike of her. But Kez, knowing there was no real need for Ali to wear it just yet, and understanding a bit more about how the transceiver worked, suspected that Raven just wanted the chance to eavesdrop on Ali and make sure that she wasn't about to betray them.

When Wraith was engrossed in watching the news on the vidscreen, his conviction that the extermination laws were wrong fueling his interest in politics, Kez brought up a question that had been worrying him.

"Raven, how are we going to make sure the CPS take Ali to that lab?" he whispered. "Why should they, when they don't even know she's a Hex?"

"I'll alter their files so they do suspect her," Raven said. "Or make an anonymous call. It'll have the same result either way. I'll do it sometime next week, it's too soon just now."

"It's a bit unfair, isn't it?" Kez said hesitantly. "It's going to wreck her whole life."

"Why should you care?" Raven shrugged. "She wouldn't care about wrecking yours."

"There isn't much she could do to make it worse," Kez said bitterly. "But she's got everything I could ever want, and we're going to take it away just like that."

"You are so strange, Kez." Raven was grinning. "Wraith thinks you're the most amoral person he's ever met but you're almost as worried about doing the right thing as him."

"Maybe because I'm not on the streets anymore," Kez pointed out. "And that's because of Wraith."

"It is?" Raven looked annoyed. "Wraith wanted to get rid of you, as I recall. It was me who let you stay."

"But now I'm here, Wraith says he won't just dump me back on the streets, and you couldn't care less about me," Kez said, before he could help himself. The fact that Raven seemed utterly uninterested in him still rankled.

"I see," Raven said slowly, studying him. Kez went red under that intense scrutiny, but then Raven turned away abruptly, picking up one of her disks and heading toward the sound system. As she loaded it into the player, she said over her shoulder: "If it makes you feel better, the CPS would have caught Ali sooner or later; she's much too careless." And with that the conversation appeared to be over. Raven had been as unaffected by his criticism as she was by Ali's or Wraith's.

Kez woke up late the next morning, light streaming in through the huge window of the room he shared with Wraith. The ganger had already left the room, presumably to get something to eat or watch the morning news. After trying for a while to get back to sleep, Kez gave up the attempt and went to stand at the window. Up in the heights of the city it was possible to be woken up by the sun. Down in gangland the shadows of the upper levels perpetually blocked out the light. If the streetlighting broke down it wasn't safe to venture outside.

Kez basked in the cold winter sunshine, looking

out at the city through the double thickness of glass, necessary in case of flitter accidents. Already the air was full of the silver streaks of metal as workers raced off to early appointments, trying to beat the traffic. The bridges were congested with skimmers, moving at a slow crawl, and Kez could even make out a few bikers weaving in and out of the traffic. No pedestrians; even up here that much hadn't changed. People only walked short distances—it took too long to navigate across the network of arches between the levels on foot.

Kez was drifting into a lazy dream, as he watched the city waking up, when suddenly a shout from the main room made him start.

"Raven, Kez! Wake up, quickly!"

"What is it?" Kez asked, as he ran out of the bedroom, ready to believe the Seccies were at the door. Wraith was staring fixedly at the vidscreen and he didn't take his gaze off it for a second as he explained:

"They've got Ali."

A reporter was babbling confusedly about a sudden shock for Bob Tarrell, owner of another news channel, and suddenly the screen filled with what was, he claimed, exclusive footage of events happening live that morning. It was the Belgravia Complex. The reporter was explaining that there had been a news team stationed there on the watch for celebrities when this extraordinary event had occurred. Behind him, Kez heard another door swish open and Raven emerged from her room, still heavy-eyed and wrapped in one of the blankets from her bed. As she saw the screen her eyes opened wide and she sat on the arm of the couch as she watched it.

Three vehicles had pulled up outside the Tarrells' apartment, including a flitter and a skimmer, both marked with the Seccies' logo. A second large unmarked flitter was with them and a group of men clustered around them. The soundtrack was explaining that this was a team of Security Services men and CPS operatives, when the door of the apartment opened and two more Seccies appeared, holding between them a confused-looking Ali. She appeared to have had time to dress and wasn't struggling with her guards. Instead she looked vacant and passively allowed herself to be manhandled into the CPS flitter. Bob Tarrell was at the door angrily demanding explanations and the Seccies were handing over papers, obviously their warrant, as the CPS operatives locked up the back of their flitter and got into it. The camera panned over from the gesticulating media magnate to focus on the plain flitter. The CPS weren't waiting for Bob Tarrell to have everything explained to him. The vehicle took off, the camera staying on it, until it had disappeared behind one of the skyrises. The reporter returned, to attempt some discreet mud-slinging and comment on the possible results of Bob Tarrell's daughter being revealed as a Hex, but Wraith muted the volume, turning to look at the others.

Kez was too astonished to think about what he was saying. Still wide-eyed with shock he exclaimed:

"How did the CPS find out she was a Hex?"

"What did you say?" Wraith demanded, taking him by the shoulders. Looking past the ganger Kez saw Raven roll her eyes, but it was too late for him to explain away his mistake.

"I . . . I . . ." he began, and stammered to a halt, frightened by Wraith's sudden anger.

"You lied, didn't you?" Wraith said, releasing Kez and swinging around to face Raven. "Both of you."

"Yes," Raven replied, meeting Wraith's eyes unashamedly.

"Whose idea was this?" Wraith asked and Kez finally managed to find the courage to speak:

"It was mine," he admitted. "The plan couldn't work without Ali, and you wouldn't have let us force her."

Wraith looked as if he wouldn't mind wringing Kez's neck for his innovative idea. But Raven's voice called him back to himself.

"What the hell does it matter, Wraith?" she asked. "It looks like we told the truth without realizing it. The CPS *have* come for Ali, without our intervention. We may have lied when we said they knew about Ali, but it turns out it was true."

"And what have they done with her?" Wraith asked, concentrating on the most important factor. "Do you know where she is?"

Raven closed her eyes, her expression becoming blank as she concentrated. This was different from entering the network through a computer. She let her consciousness rove through the living city, searching for a signal which she alone could recognize. Wraith's presence next to her was confusing, his own transceiver gave out the same signal, and it was difficult to search for another one. She concentrated, trying to distinguish the tracking device which would locate Ali from the multitude of electronic signals buzzing through the ether. A minute passed, slowly, then her eyes snapped open.

"They're heading out of London," she said. "Toward the north."

"Are they taking her to the lab?" Wraith demanded. "Or are they taking her for extermination?"

"I think the lab," Raven said. "There are extermination facilities in London."

"Check," Wraith said coldly. "We don't want to make a mistake."

"OK." Raven didn't argue. She walked over to the wall terminal, still wrapped in her blanket, and let her hands rest on the keypad. Wraith and Kez waited, for over five minutes this time, until Raven's eyes focused again and she looked up from the terminal. "It's the laboratory," she stated. "Those operatives are ordered to hand Ali over to Dr. Kalden, just as Rachel was."

"Can you speak to her?" Wraith asked. "Is the transceiver working?"

"It's working," Raven replied. "But I can't contact her—if the CPS pick up the transmission we'd be endangering ourselves as well as Ali."

"All right." Wraith nodded grimly. "I want you to keep in constant contact with Ali's transceiver. Tell me when you find out exactly where the lab is, but don't lose contact. I want you to know what's happening to her every minute."

"Wraith, stay chill . . ." Raven began, but Wraith didn't let her finish.

"I don't want to hear it, Raven," he said coldly. "You were responsible for trying to get Ali caught by the CPS. Now she has been and you're to make sure that nothing worse happens to her." He looked at Kez. "And you can stay with her—try and be useful." Then he turned and headed for the main door to the suite. "I'm going to get something to eat."

"Well, that went down well," Raven said sarcastically as the door closed behind Wraith. "I think he's losing sight of the main issue here. Does he want to rescue Rachel, or not?" She shrugged one shoulder and turned back to the terminal as Kez miserably sat down to watch her.

The flitter coasted through the skies, over the sprawling suburbs, and out toward the north. It would have been difficult for Ali to tell where the city ended and the country began, as the congested freeway below them was bordered by industrial development. But the back of the flitter was shielded in any case, with no way for her to see where she was going.

She had been pushed onto a steel bench with restraints that fixed around her wrists holding her to it. Two CPS operatives, a man and a woman, sat facing her, as if unwilling to contaminate themselves with closer association. The inside of the flitter was stripped of all other equipment, and a thick shield separated the back of the vehicle from the control console in the front.

Ali was shaking, clutching the bench she was locked to. She kept her head down, unable to look at the CPS agents. But even more than terror, the emotion that overwhelmed her was shame. She had seen the camera crew filming her humiliation as she was dragged out of the door of her apartment and all she could think of was what Zircarda and Caitlin would say, watching the news together. But what hurt the most had been her father's reaction. When he had called her out of her room, she had thought at first he had found out about her visit to the Stratos the day before. But then she had seen the five uniformed men standing by the main door of the apartment and knew with a horrified realization that they had come for her. Her father had looked at her with a mixture of disappointment and fear. It was the fear that had made her start to shake. He had never looked at her with anything other than affection and tolerance. She wasn't really clever enough to earn his admiration— her school record had always been average at best— but he had always been fond of her without that. To have him be afraid of her was something Ali had never envisaged.

The Seccies had told her to get dressed quickly and one of them, a woman, had stayed with her while she did so. Once she was dressed the woman took her back into the main room, where one of the other Seccies was examining the computer terminals. Another immediately sealed the door of her room and attached an SS classification to it. It was only then that Bob had begun to recover his composure.

"What is this?" he demanded. "What's going to happen to my daughter?"

"Your daughter is a suspected Hex, Mr. Tarrell,"

one of the officers said emotionlessly. "She will be taken for evaluation and when the mutation is confirmed, she will be disposed of." Ali felt a hysterical laugh building inside her as the man used the same term that Wraith had criticized her for using. She clamped down hard on it, holding her mouth tight shut.

"And what if she isn't a Hex?" her father was saying.

"If that is the case she will be returned to you before the end of the day," the man told him. "But it is rarely the case that a person is suspected incorrectly. Extermination is scheduled for this evening."

Her father had looked so stunned that Ali had wanted to tell him what Wraith and Raven had found out about the laboratory, that there was a good chance she would be taken there. But she knew that telling him that would mean she would be exterminated for certain and kept silent. She felt dazed as two Seccies took her out of the apartment, barely hearing her father's protests. The men had bundled her into the flitter, handing her over to two CPS operatives who had checked her for concealed weapons before locking her into the restraints. Ali had felt horribly conscious of the transceiver ear-stud, which she hadn't removed the night before. But the CPS people didn't even seem to notice it. As the flitter took off, Ali prayed that Raven was tracking her. Despite the fact that it was Wraith she trusted and Wraith who was the leader of the group, it was Raven who held her life in her hands.

Ali thought of Raven with all her might as the flitter sped on. She remembered what the girl had told her in the hotel: "Concentrate on the fact that I'm going to be saving your life." She had meant it as a warning, Ali was certain, to prevent any more criticism of her motives. But now Ali recalled it as a promise. The CPS had no idea of how far Raven's powers extended. They didn't even know she existed. And for whatever reasons, whether to save Rachel or satisfy a morbid curiosity, Raven would be watching out for her. It was the only hope Ali had and she clung to it.

7

Nature's Mischief

The room Ali had been left in was plain and windowless, and something like a private room at a hospital. There was a single bed and some equipment to monitor life-signs and brainwaves, standing near it. But it contained no computer equipment. There was also a small metal table and a single chair, both bolted to the floor. Apart from that the room was empty. Lying on the bed were the white overalls Ali had been told to put on, made of a thin material. But somehow her own clothes seemed like her last link with home and she made no move to change, sitting hunched against the wall.

There was no lock on the door and it had a large pane of shatter-proof glass set into it, as if to emphasize the complete lack of privacy. Under the circumstances Ali had made no move to close the door, which the CPS operatives had left open—it would have been a pointless exercise. So she was surprised when she heard a quiet knock, although she didn't move from her position against the wall. There was a pause, and then she heard the door swing further open as someone entered the room.

"Are you OK?" a voice asked.

Ali looked up then, if only to tell the speaker exactly what she thought of such an utterly stupid and pointless question. But she was arrested by the sight that awaited her. It was a boy, perhaps about her age, but she found it hard to tell for certain. He was painfully thin, almost emaciated, and his white overalls hung off his scarecrow figure like rags. The sleeves of the overalls were short enough for Ali to see the yellow bruises that covered his arms, like those of a drug-user. He saw her looking and his mouth pulled into a travesty of a smile.

"My name's Luciel," he told her. "They're testing to see if drugs break my connection with electronics. I guess they haven't found the right formula yet."

"I'm Ali," she said, standing up awkwardly, and glancing at the open door. "Are we allowed to talk?"

"We pretty much do what we want to," the boy said. "Unless someone's door is guarded. That means they're doing experiments."

"Who exactly are *they*?" Ali asked, although she could already guess the answer.

"The scientists," Luciel replied uneasily.

"Is one of them called Dr. Kalden?"

"Shhh," Luciel warned, suddenly alarmed. "We don't talk about them, and especially not about *him*." He tried to smile again. "I came to see you because I knew you'd be scared, everyone is. But it helps that we're allowed to talk to each other."

"Yes, it does," Ali admitted. She hesitated. "Can I ask you another question?"

"OK," Luciel replied slowly.

"Is there a girl called Rachel here?" Ali asked. "She's a . . . a friend of mine. About eleven years old, brown hair, brown eyes . . ."

"I'm sorry." Luciel shook his head. "I can't think of anyone like that." Ali's heart sank; everything felt cut from under her. But then Luciel added, "But there are a lot of people here and I don't know them all. Your friend could still be here."

Despite Luciel's claim that they were allowed to go anywhere they wanted, the boy seemed unwilling to venture out into the rest of the laboratory, although he did his best to make Ali feel resigned to her new situation. He was very different from Raven. Not only did he lack her magnetism and self-confidence, he was generally much more uncertain about himself and his own abilities. After the contempt Raven had shown toward Ali's two ventures into the net she had thought herself a novice. But, according to Luciel, no one in the facility had much more experience than that either.

However, Ali did not describe Raven to him as an example. She steered clear of the entire subject of the gangers. After all she didn't know who could be trusted in this place and, even more, she was beginning to feel guilty about the whole situation. She had been thinking of her venture into the lab almost as a game, but people here were being experimented on, in ways that she could only guess at. Anything she imagined could only be guesswork, as Luciel was unwilling to tell her anything about the experimentation.

"It's better not to know," he said when she demanded he enlighten her further.

"How can I not know?" she asked. "They're going to be experimenting on me, aren't they?"

"But not for a while," Luciel replied uncomfortably. "First they run a whole lot of tests, to try to find out your capabilities, stuff like that. It's only when they've found out as much as they can that the scientists really start experimenting."

"Do they always do . . . what they've done to you?" Ali found it difficult to look at Luciel's bruised arms.

"No . . ." he said reluctantly. "They do different things to different people. You'll see when you meet the others."

"OK, then." Ali made a motion as if to leave the room, but Luciel shook his head.

"You can't yet," he told her. "Not until they've examined you."

"Is that a rule?" Ali asked.

"No, it's . . . it's . . . it's just the way things are." Luciel shrugged his thin shoulders. "They'll probably be here soon," he said. "I'd better go. Good luck, Ali." He paused just before leaving the room. "You'd better put the overalls on," he told her, "just so as not to annoy them."

Ali changed into the white overalls. It wasn't so much Luciel's words that had affected her as the haunted look in his eyes. She wondered miserably what she had got herself into and, sitting slumped on the bed, felt bitterly angry with the gangers who had got her into all this.

"I wish I'd never met that *bitch!*" she said under her breath and gave a convulsive start when a voice in her ears answered:

"Do you mean me?"

"Raven!" Ali exclaimed. "You can hear me?"

"That is what this device is for," Raven reminded her, the Hex's voice reverberating in Ali's ears. *"According to the transmitter, you are alone and there are no monitoring devices in the room."*

"Did you hear my conversation with Luciel?" Ali asked.

"The transmitter can pick up any sounds within a ten-meter radius."

"Then you heard what he said about Rachel," Ali said, "that she might not be here."

"I'm not an idiot," Raven said caustically. *"I have always been aware of the possibility that Rachel is already dead. But you'll have to meet the other people being held to find out for sure."* There was a short silence, and Ali wondered if Raven had signed off before she heard the girl's voice again. *"Are you OK?"*

"I can't believe you'd be concerned," Ali told her. There was a longer silence. This time Ali knew Raven was still there and she waited for the reply, wondering what the girl would come out with this time. But Raven's answer, when it finally came, surprised her.

"I don't like the sound of that lab," she said. *"I wouldn't like to be in your place."*

"I'm afraid," Ali admitted, disarmed by Raven's unexpected empathy.

"I'll be in constant contact," Raven told her, adding ironically, *"I don't know if you'll find that a comfort."*

"If something happens ... if they start experimenting on me," Ali asked quietly, "will you get me out of here?" She dreaded the answer, wondered if she had asked too much too soon. Raven didn't have her brother's moral code, and even if the loyalty of the group lay with him, she held the sum of the power. It was Raven's support she needed. She didn't expect the younger girl to react with sympathy—that would have been too much to ask. But Raven hadn't exaggerated when she said she didn't like the sound of the lab.

"I'll tell Wraith we should get into position," she said eventually. *"Just in case."*

Kez glanced up in surprise as Raven disengaged herself from the terminal. She had been speaking softly into its audio pick-up, too quietly for him to overhear. But now she got up from her chair and stretched her aching muscles. She was still wearing the baggy gray sweater, sweatpants and thick socks she had slept in; the blanket lay discarded on the floor beside the computer terminal. Kez had left his silent vigil to get dressed, but Raven had been glued to the terminal for the past three hours, and had looked up only once to tell him that Ali had arrived at the lab.

Now she stretched her legs to get some feeling back into them, flexing her fingers experimentally.

"Is Wraith back yet?" she asked.

"He came back about an hour ago," Kez told her, easily able to believe that her intense concentration had blocked out her brother's presence. It wasn't as if Wraith had said anything to either of them. "But he went out again, almost right away."

"I see," Raven said and stretched again. "God, I really need a shower."

"Wraith didn't want you to leave the terminal," Kez cautioned her.

"I'm still in contact," Raven told him. "It's harder without the net to rely on, but it can be done." She rubbed her shoulders, wincing a little. "I feel awful," she complained, and glanced back at Kez, "and you look worse."

"Wraith's really angry," he said, looking down at the ground.

"He'll get over it—relax," Raven advised. "I've spoken to Ali," she added.

"Is she OK?" Kez asked guiltily.

"She seems to be." Raven wrinkled her nose. "But she wants to be sure that we can break her out if we need to. We'd better get moving. When Wraith gets back tell him to get ready to leave. I'll call the Countess and make sure our transport's ready."

"Why can't *you* tell Wraith?" Kez protested, wary of speaking to the ganger in his current mood.

"Because I'm going to take a shower," Raven said definitively and left the room.

The scientists came not long after Ali had spoken to Raven. The two Hexes hadn't had much to say to each other, their brief rapport had been too tenuous for that. But Ali did find it comforting to think that Raven was monitoring her over the transceiver link, even though that didn't help much when she was confronted with the reality of the scientists.

In actual fact the examination wasn't that different from the check-ups her doctor gave her, although it was a little more extensive. She was examined by a woman scientist in a spotless white lab coat wearing a face mask and thin transparent gloves over her hands, while another woman took down details on paper. Obviously the CPS weren't risking the chance of a Hex getting linked up to a computer. Two regular CPS operatives, without lab coats, stood guard outside the door while Ali was examined. It took over an hour for the scientists to get all the results they needed, linking Ali up to most of the scanners in the room to perform some of the more complex tests.

Finally the woman who had been running tests on Ali stepped back and went to look at her companion's clipboard.

"That's the lot, isn't it?" she said, in an undertone.

"Everything," the second scientist replied. "I'd better take these results to be processed. Once we have the confirmation of the genetic scan, we can send out the notification of death to the family."

"Fine," the first scientist nodded, then she looked back at Ali and addressed her as if she was an imbecile, enunciating every syllable: "We have finished examining you," she said. "Meals will be brought to you twice a day. You may interact with the other test-subjects if you wish. There is a clearly signed washing room, for the use of the subjects on this corridor,

three doors away from this room. We will return
when it is time for your second series of tests. If you
are obedient and not obstructive you will be treated
well." Then both scientists left the room, taking Ali's
discarded clothes with them in a sealed plastic bag.
Ali could hear the booted footsteps of the guards following them away down the corridor.

Once they had gone she reached up to touch the
white ear-stud in her right ear. It had been concealed
by her hair for most of the examination, but the few
times when it must have been seen the scientist had
paid no attention. She had seemed reluctant even to
look at Ali, plainly considering her on a par with an
unpleasant micro-virus she had been ordered to test.
It was a new experience for the spoiled rich kid from
Belgravia, and one that Ali was anxious to forget.

Walking to the door of the room, she looked out at
the corridor. It was plain and white, stretching for
quite a long way. No one was visible in either direction and Ali left the room cautiously. She could see
doors set into the walls at regular intervals. One had
a sign on it marked *Washing Room*. At one end of the
corridor was an elevator; at the other end was a set of
double doors with large panes of shatter-proof glass
set into them. Ali walked toward the end of the corridor with the doors in it, resisting the urge to look
into the rooms she passed on either side. When she
reached the doors, she pushed them open gingerly.
There wasn't much to see. Another corridor stretched
out, again in two directions, double doors at both
ends. Halfway up this second corridor was another
washing room.

Ali felt any desire to explore further leeched out of her by the featureless, institutionalized atmosphere of the facility. She wondered how she would ever find Rachel. But she supposed she had better try. Returning to her own corridor, she walked down to the elevator. There was an unmarked touchpad beside it. Ali didn't have the nerve to press it. Instead she began to methodically work her way down the corridor, looking in each of the rooms. They were all marked with a short code sequence, but the codes didn't seem to be arranged in any order.

At first Ali's curiosity was not indulged. The first three rooms were all empty and apparently unoccupied, not even containing the medical equipment she had found in her own. The fourth was also unoccupied, but the room was full of medical scanners; like the other equipment Ali had seen in the lab they had no computer interface. The bed was unmade and an untouched tray of food lay on the small table. The tray was plastic and divided up into sections, each of which held a puréed substance of different colors. The only utensil was a metal spoon. It was the most unappetizing meal Ali had ever seen; she wasn't surprised that it had been left uneaten. Moving on she looked through the window of the next room.

A child lay unconscious on the bed, linked up to the machines that surrounded it. Tubes were connected to his mouth and nose, and monitors were attached to his wrists and forehead. He didn't look more than six or seven years old. Going into the room to look at him more closely, Ali felt as if she was desecrating a tomb, one of the cemeteries that

still existed in parts of Europe, unusable for farm-
land or industrial expansion. The boy was like the
living dead, lying in the midst of a mass of machinery, like a fly in the web of a mechanical spider.

She heard footsteps behind her as someone else
entered the room and she turned to see Luciel, meeting his shadowed eyes contritely.

"This is why I didn't want you to look around,
just yet," he told her. "It's hard to take, at first."

"Are a lot of people like this?" Ali asked.

"Some," Luciel replied. "Not everyone's as bad as
this, though." He bit his lips before adding: "A few
are worse."

"What could be worse than this?" Ali asked in
horror and realized almost instantaneously that she
didn't want to know.

"We don't talk about it," Luciel said. Not looking
at the boy on the bed, he headed out of the room. Ali
followed him and waited as he closed the door behind them.

"What's his name?" she asked.

"I'm not sure," Luciel shrugged. "Does it matter?
Jack or Jesse, something like that. He used to cry at
night and he wet the bed. And he was always asking
questions."

"Don't you care?" Ali asked incredulously, and
she felt like Wraith.

"I don't know." Luciel met her eyes unashamedly.
"Is it wrong to be glad it's not me?"

"I'm not sure." Ali thought for a while, leaning up
against the corridor wall. "I think I'd feel the same
way. But . . . I have a friend, a sort of friend, who said

that the reason Hexes didn't help each other was that anyone clever enough to escape the CPS wouldn't care about someone who got caught. I was angry with her for thinking that way, because she only cares about herself."

"Was she a Hex?" Luciel asked softly, checking to see that they weren't being overheard.

"Yes," whispered Ali, wondering if Raven was listening, and what the girl would say later if she was.

"And she hasn't been caught?" Luciel asked, even more quietly if it was possible.

"No," Ali replied.

"Then maybe she was right to think that way," Luciel said. "I didn't and I was caught. If it would have changed anything I'd have been as selfish as I could."

Ali didn't say anything, but inwardly she resolved that she wouldn't be leaving the lab alone, even if she didn't manage to find Rachel. Now that she'd seen two other inmates, she felt guilty at the thought of leaving without them. She realized what Wraith had meant about the callousness of the experimentation; just a few hours in the lab had convinced her that he was right. But the thought of Rachel recalled her to the fact that she had a mission.

When Ali reminded Luciel that she wanted to find someone, he was perfectly willing to help.

"It's not as if there's anything else to do here," he pointed out. "There's nothing to read, and nothing to see. We don't get access to vidscreens, and God forbid that we should even *look* at a computer terminal."

"Do you know if there's a main computer control room?" Ali asked as casually as she could.

"I guess there must be," Luciel replied, puzzled. "But if there is, we'd never get the chance to see it."

"I guess not," Ali agreed. Looking down the long corridor, she felt apprehensive. "How many people are there here?"

"Hundreds, I think," Luciel said, adding: "But people keep dying, and they bring in new Hexes all the time. Mostly kids."

"Is everyone a Hex?" Ali asked, remembering Raven's insistence that the CPS had got it wrong. "Definitely a Hex?"

"I guess so," Luciel said. "No one who comes here is ever sent back home again, anyhow."

When Wraith returned to the hotel suite Kez was packing up the electronic equipment.

"What are you doing?" he asked immediately. "Where's Raven?"

"She's spoken to Ali," Kez said, trying to choose the response least likely to annoy Wraith. "She thinks it's time to get closer to the lab; Ali wants us to be ready to break in if she gets into any trouble."

"I can't believe that Raven would care about that," Wraith said sarcastically. "Or that you do, come to think of it."

"I don't want anything to happen to Ali," Kez said, carefully packing up the home-made explosives.

"You surprise me," Wraith said coldly and Kez felt a sudden flash of anger. He felt that Wraith was treating him unfairly, especially considering that he had lied for him, so he could find his sister.

"Why do I surprise you?" he asked. "You told Raven you'd never known anyone with fewer morals, so how can you be surprised that I lied to you?"

Wraith met Kez's eyes.

"Maybe because I wanted to trust you," he said. "I tend to automatically suspect Raven's advice because I don't understand her motivations. But I thought I did understand you."

"Because there isn't much to understand?" Kez asked.

"Because you're not so different from the gangers I knew in Denver," Wraith told him. He studied Kez for a while. "I can guess why you lied, Kez, and this time I'll forget it. But don't do it again. I have to be able to trust someone, and this group is so mismatched that it really has to be you."

"Does that mean you want the group to stay together?" Kez asked, considering how such an intention would affect him.

"Perhaps, if we're successful in breaking Rachel and Ali out of the lab."

"OK, then." Kez had made his decision. "You can trust me."

Wraith nodded, although he still wasn't sure if he could believe Kez's promise. He began crating up the rest of the gear they would need to take with them, deliberately ignoring Raven's heaps of lasdisks. Now that Ali was inside the lab the operation had become too serious for his sister's eccentricity.

Raven emerged from her room before he was finished, obviously ready to leave. She didn't look very different from when she had first arrived in the gangland slum district. But instead of her jacket she was carrying a long coat, one of her more recent acquisitions, which she began to load with some of the smaller and more complex pieces of electrical equipment.

"The Countess has transport and muscle back-up waiting," she told Wraith. "We'll need a combat weapon of some kind for Kez."

"Can you use a gun?" Wraith asked the boy and Kez shrugged.

"I'm better with a knife."

"Too risky," Raven said, echoing Wraith's unspoken thoughts. "You won't get close enough to use it."

"I'll show you how to operate a laser pistol," Wraith said. "It sights automatically and it burns rather than blasts."

"Is that what you carry?" Kez asked the ganger and Raven grinned.

"It's generally regarded as a breach of etiquette to ask a ganger that question," she informed him.

"Since we're going in on this raid together, it's best to know what kind of fire-power each of us has," Wraith pointed out. "I have been carrying a laser pistol but I think breaking into the lab will require something heavier. I'll get that from the Countess and you can use my pistol."

"What about Raven?" Kez asked curiously, eyeing the deep inner pockets of the girl's long coat, into which her tools had disappeared.

"Keep guessing," she told him, with a sideways glance at Wraith. Kez looked inquiringly at the ganger.

"I don't even know if she carries weapons," he

said. "Is there anything you want from the Countess, Raven?"

"If there is, I'll deal with it myself," she said. "But don't worry about how I'll defend myself, Wraith. This isn't the first time I've been part of this kind of operation." She smiled slightly, but didn't say anything more, and neither Wraith nor Kez asked anything else.

They left the hotel suite half an hour after Wraith's return, once the skimmer was loaded with what they would need to attack the lab. Raven dealt with checking out of the Stratos, paying from one of the immense credit balances she had persuaded a bank to give her. She also arranged to have her disk collection packaged up and sent to Bob Tarrell, with the compliments of AdAstra. Wraith had refused to take it with them and Raven, now that she was no longer suffering from the monotony of the search, didn't really feel the need to surround herself with high-decibel rock music.

However, she did retain a few disks, so that as the skimmer wound its way down through the levels of the city, a pounding backbeat filled the vehicle. Raven drove fast, bringing back memories for Kez of the sickening trip she had sent the flitter on when he first encountered her. Wraith sat in a grim silence, mentally checking and rechecking his plans. He was very aware of the fact that Ali was in Kalden's laboratory and felt that it was his responsibility to get her out again. Too many people had died already for him to sacrifice Ali for a chance to save Rachel.

Ali had begun to dread finding Rachel. It had been made clear to her that anyone who'd been in

the lab for over a year was unlikely to be found un-
damaged. And some of the experiments being performed in the lab were horrific. Luciel had actually
been one of the luckier ones. The CPS scientists had
used their imagination to the utmost when devising
experiments to test the capabilities of the child Hexes
brought into the lab. On Ali's floor alone there
seemed to be endless corridors of test-subjects and
she had no idea what might lie above or below. Luciel had informed her that the elevator was restricted
to laboratory staff and had no more idea than her of
the actual size of the facility.

Ali hadn't found Rachel among the children, and
any kind of methodical search was proving difficult.
She had first ventured out of her room when the others were having the first of the two meals of the day,
served at midmorning. But before long the silent corridors were very different. The younger children
seemed relentlessly hyperactive and antisocial, racing down the corridors and banging into anyone
who got in their way. Then a lot of the older ones
were unwilling even to speak to Luciel, let alone Ali,
and there were many who were unable to speak.
They were forced to progress slowly and Ali was
grateful that Luciel had agreed to help her, since
most of the other test-subjects regarded her with suspicion. Her companion explained it as jealousy, that
she hadn't been subjected to the methods of the scientists' endless quest for knowledge. His bruised
arms and jerky, uncertain movements were almost a
badge of honor in the facility and Ali discovered that
he had been there longer than most people.

"Two and a half years," he told her with resignation. "I think my immune system is becoming resistant to the drugs they keep testing on me. A lot of the others died from the course of injections."

"If you've been here that long you must have seen Rachel brought in," Ali said and Luciel sighed.

"I don't notice everyone," he said. "It's only recently I've been trying to meet new inmates, and I don't always realize when they're bringing in someone new. Besides there could be other floors full of us. Believe me, Ali, if I knew anything about your friend I'd tell you."

"I know," Ali said, trusting him absolutely. Luciel was trying hard to help her find Rachel. Since their search of the corridors was proving impossible, he took her to meet other people who might know when the girl had been brought in and if she was still there.

The first person he took her to find was, he explained, difficult to deal with. But he had been at the lab nearly as long as Luciel and might know something about Rachel. Thomas's initial reaction to Ali's presence was not positive.

"What do you want?" he asked gruffly, when Luciel knocked at the open door of his room. He was a stocky teenager, at least as old as Ali, built like a wrestler. But he didn't stand up to greet them, watching suspiciously from where he sat on his bed. His thick, muscular frame was concealed by what appeared to be body armor strapped to his arms and legs. Smooth white metal enclosed his shins and ankles in a vise-like grip, similar devices were attached to his forearms and wrists, two more ringed his torso and encircled his neck. He looked almost robotic, so thoroughly encased in metal. Thomas saw her looking and glared.

"What are you staring at?" he demanded and got to his feet. His movements were heavy and ponderous and there was a mechanical purr from the devices strapped to his legs.

"Calm down, Tom," Luciel said placatingly. "Ali's only just arrived. She's trying to find a friend of hers, a little girl." He spoke quickly, as if to avert sudden violence, and the ferocious expression on Thomas's face gradually smoothed out.

"Don't stare at me," he told Ali, who flushed, retreating a little behind Luciel.

"Sorry," she mumbled uncomfortably.

"Just wait till they start taking you apart," Thomas told her roughly. "You won't be looking so cool then." He clenched a fist, enclosed in a metal mesh, and electronics hummed audibly. "I *hate* that noise," he told her fiercely. "I try to lie still at night so I won't have to hear it. They've made it so I don't even want to move anymore, but when they come to check on me I have to. They take me up in the elevator and make me walk round a room while they watch me. Do you know what that feels like?"

"I'm sorry," Ali said again, but couldn't quell the flood of bitterness emanating from Tom.

"I used to play basketball at school," he told her. "I was gonna be a professional. Not much chance of that now, is there?"

"I was going to be a scientist," Luciel said quietly and Ali shivered.

"I wanted to be a holovid director," she said, realizing that, even if she did escape from the lab, that would never happen now.

They all stood still, looking at each other. Thomas was the first to break the silence.

"What was that you were saying earlier?" he asked Luciel.

"Oh." Luciel came back to earth abruptly. "Ali's looking for a friend, a girl named Rachel. She was captured by the CPS about a year and a half ago. We were hoping you might remember someone like that coming into the lab."

"What does she look like?" Tom asked and Ali tried to visualize the picture Wraith had shown her.

"Dark brown hair in a short bob, brown eyes, light brown skin, a big smile," she recited.

"If she was brought here she wouldn't be smiling long," Tom said and then shook his head. "No, I don't remember her. But wasn't it about then that they were doing memory experiments?" He looked at Luciel rather than at Ali and the other boy's eyes clouded.

"It might have been," he said. "I find it hard to keep track of time sometimes."

"What were the memory experiments?" Ali asked, with an ominous feeling.

"They only went on for a couple of months," Tom told her. "They were abandoned because almost everyone who was experimented on died." Ali blanched and Luciel shot a warning look at Thomas, taking up the narrative himself.

"They linked up a group of kids to a computer database," he said, "with electrodes so they couldn't disengage themselves, and ran it twenty-four hours a day." He thought for a second. "I think the idea was to find out how much information a Hex could hold in their head, since a lot of us have eidetic memories."

"What happened?" Ali managed to ask, finding her voice again.

"Most people did die, I'm afraid," Luciel admitted, more gently than his friend had. "But two or three are still around—one of them might be able to tell you if Rachel was on the project."

"You're kidding yourself," Tom told him, raising his voice a little to cover the drone of machinery as he moved back to his bed. "None of those flakes will be telling you anything."

"Why not?" Ali asked. Luciel wouldn't look at her and she turned back to Tom.

"They're complete null-brainers," he said callously. "Esther sits in her room dribbling and playing with her food, Mikhail's covered in more machinery than I am and Revenge has to be strapped to her bed with restraints because otherwise she tries to claw your eyes out." He paused to see how his words had affected Ali and seemed satisfied with her expression because he continued: "None of them'll tell you anything because they won't tolerate anyone anywhere near 'em, and even if they were willing to, their brains are too fritzed to remember what happened yesterday, let alone the name of some girl who might not even have been sent here in the first place."

"I'm sorry, Ali," Luciel said softly. "Tom's right. If Rachel was part of those experiments, she's lucky to be dead."

8

Hell Is Murky

Kez had a feeling of *déjà vu* as the skimmer coasted along the last bridge and came to rest near the spur of walkway that led to the Countess's center of operations, where she traded information and abilities. Kez moved to unfasten his seat belt but Wraith forestalled him.

"Wait," he said. "Someone should stay and guard the skimmer. We need this stuff."

"OK," Kez said, trying hard not to remember what had been the outcome of his last attempt at watching a vehicle for Wraith. "But what can I do if someone does try to steal it?"

"Don't confront them," Raven said. "They won't be able to unlock the doors anyway." She got out of the driver's seat and Wraith followed her example. Sitting in the front of the vehicle, Kez felt a little abandoned as they set off toward the building together. But, before they were completely out of sight,

Raven turned and waved. Wraith, in what appeared to be a demonstration of trust, didn't look back at all.

This time Wraith wasn't challenged as he approached the building. When he entered, it looked like it hadn't changed at all since his last visit. However, only one of the two guards from last time, the woman, stood in front of the door which led upstairs.

"Names and business," she demanded, although her eyes showed recognition as she glanced at Wraith.

"Wraith and Raven," the ganger said, addressing the vidcom screen on the wall beside the guard. "The Countess knows my business already."

"You may come up," the voice spoke out of the wall unit. "Leave your weapons behind."

"OK," Wraith agreed, obediently handing over his laser pistol and one of his knives. The guard accepted them and turned expectantly to Raven.

"No," Raven told her and the guard shifted her grip on the combat rifle she carried.

"Do you have some reason for objecting?" the Countess asked, from the vidcom, although the screen was still blacked out.

"Just caution," Raven told her, with a shrug. "If I have to disarm, I'd rather stay down here."

"In some cases I am willing to make exceptions," the Countess said dryly, "and I am willing to make one for you. But any trouble and you won't know what hit you."

"I scan," Raven said, slipping into the gangland argot that seemed to overtake her in the slums.

"Go ahead," the guard said, with a sour look at Raven, stepping aside for them to pass by.

Wraith was curious to see how his sister would react to the disorienting stairway with its mirror shielding, and noticed her expression of distaste as she ascended beside him. She walked as slowly and carefully as he did, disliking the loss of balance that the multiple reflections engendered.

"Effective, isn't it?" he said, and she gave him a sideways glance.

"Narcissistic," she said. "But I'd like to know what's behind it. Shielding like this could conceal anything, motion sensors, monitors, transmitters, maybe a few explosives just in case." Her cold smile was multiplied in every direction. "It seems as if you've found a good contact, though."

"I hope so," Wraith replied as they reached the top of the stairs and the mirrored wall slid away.

The Countess was waiting for them, watching with interest as they entered. Raven's dark eyes flickered over the screens and terminals that filled the room before coming to rest on the woman herself with the intensity that often alarmed people. The Countess returned her gaze speculatively.

"You must be a technician as well as a hacker, if you could guess all that about my shielding," she said. "Is that why you wouldn't give up your weapons?"

"Good guess," Raven replied, with a grin. "I'm not biting."

"I don't like customized weaponry," the Countess told her matter-of-factly. "Always lets you down when you really need it. Makes me think it's a bad idea to tinker with it."

"I don't tinker," Raven said in annoyance, stung into a rejoinder. The Countess's expression brightened and Raven narrowed her eyes in response, disliking the way she was being manipulated.

"Your transport's ready, Wraith," the Countess continued. "I'll have it brought into the building. I've got muscle for you as well but the main question is where you want to take them. You originally contacted me to locate your sister's adoptive parents and you claimed then you weren't planning a retrieval. Since I ascertained the whereabouts of the Hollis family, you have bought some heavy artillery and now you want muscle as well. I doubt that you are intending to break into the Hollises' apartment with quite that much firepower."

"Rachel wasn't at the apartment," Wraith admitted cautiously, keeping an eye on Raven. "I want to retrieve her from the place she is now."

"Which is?" The Countess waited, her stance making it clear that no further business could be done without an answer.

"A laboratory run by the CPS," Raven said suddenly.

"Then she's a Hex," the Countess stated definitively.

"It would appear so," Raven agreed, not entirely willing to concede the point.

"And what about you?" the Countess asked. "Your brother told me on our first meeting that you were a hacker. Are you a Hex as well?"

"If I was I would hardly admit it," Raven pointed out.

"I imagine not," the Countess agreed. "And it would be bad for business if my clients lost faith in my discretion." She waited for Raven's nod of assent before continuing. "However, this development does entail that your back-up is equally discreet. That means a higher fee and I can't guarantee they'll agree to this kind of work. Not all of my contacts would be sanguine about breaking into a CPS facility to rescue a Hex."

Ali was lying on the hard hospital bed trying to think. Ever since she had parted from Luciel she had been trying to work out what to do and how Rachel's death would affect the group. But her mind had been a confusion of impressions and ideas, and thinking was difficult in the abattoir-like laboratory. She felt almost able to see the mutilated children behind the walls in the rooms on her corridor, the other corridors on that floor and all the others who had ever occupied the laboratory, no matter how briefly.

On the small table lay the remains of the food tray that had been brought to her late that afternoon. Two uniformed operatives had wheeled trolleys down the hallway, ordering children out of their rooms to collect their trays. A scientist, following behind, had adjusted the intravenous feeding-tubes of those confined to their beds. Ali had accepted her tray obediently, but hadn't been able to stomach more than a few mouthfuls of the tasteless substances that passed for food.

With a sigh, Ali sat up. She was getting nowhere trying to work this out on her own. Cautiously, almost furtively, she moved to the door of her room on silent bare feet. There was no one outside. She shut the door, wishing there was some way to cover the see-through opening, and returned to the bed. This time she lay on her stomach so no one looking in would be able to see her face. Then, hoping that this would work, she whispered:

"Raven?"

There was no answer. Ali felt like crying. Digging her nails hard into the palms of her hands, using the pain to block out her despair, she tried again. It was almost like praying, she thought hysterically, as she whispered Raven's name into the silence of her room. Trying to contact someone who might not be listening.

"Raven, can you hear me?" Ali was losing hope. "Raven, if you're there, please answer me . . . please . . ."

"I can hear you. What's happening?" a cool voice answered and Ali felt almost numb with relief.

"I need to talk to you," she said quickly. "A lot's happened."

"I'm here," Raven told her, *"and there's nothing that requires my immediate attention elsewhere. So, why do you feel this sudden need for conversation?"*

"It's horrible here," Ali said, but strangely, the sound of Raven's voice, unchanged and slightly sarcastic, was comforting. It reassured her that there was a world outside the laboratory and that she was still in contact with it.

"*What do you mean by 'horrible'?*" Raven asked slowly.

"The scientists have been performing the most gruesome experiments on people," Ali said. "There's a boy who's had all his nerves destroyed. He can only move by sending electrical impulses to the machinery they've strapped around his body, and Luciel gets injected with drugs all the time, to try to block the parts of his brain that make him a Hex, and . . ."

"*Cool it, Ali,*" Raven said suddenly. "*You sound hysterical. Get it together.*"

"Don't tell me that," Ali gasped. "You're not the one who's stuck here. How can I be calm? They could be coming to get me any time!"

"*They haven't even processed your test results yet,*" Raven said firmly.

"How do you know that?" Ali demanded. "I thought you couldn't even contact the computer system here."

"*I still can't,*" Raven said. "*But I listened in while you were examined this morning, and the scientists said that when your results had been processed a death certificate would be sent to your father. Well, he hasn't been notified yet—I've checked his terminal—and even when he has been you have at least one more set of tests to go.*" She waited for a while for Ali to regain control of herself. "*Now, are you calm?*" she asked.

"I'm calm," Ali replied, with a little irritation. "Now will you listen to me?"

"*I'm listening,*" Raven said with exaggerated patience and Ali launched into an account of the day's events.

Raven listened in silence for a while—at least Ali presumed she was still listening—but when it came to the reference to memory experiments she interrupted, insisting that Ali recount the conversation in more detail. Unwillingly, Ali told her everything that Tom had said about the only survivors of the experiments. When she had finished there was a long silence.

"Are you still there?" she asked, somewhat dubiously.

"Yes, I'm still here," Raven replied. *"Shut up and let me think."*

"OK, OK," Ali told her and waited.

"What were their names?" Raven said eventually.

"The kids in the memory experiments?" Ali asked. "I told you that."

"Tell me again," Rachel insisted. *"Their names."*

"I think Tom said they were called Mikhail, Esther and Revenge," Ali said. "I can check with him, though."

"No, there's no need," Raven said. *"But I want you to try and see them."*

"It won't do any good," Ali protested. "Luciel agreed with Tom—they wouldn't remember anything about Rachel."

"Ali, go and see them," Raven ordered.

"Why?" Ali objected.

"Because I have a . . . a hunch," Raven said, almost uncertainly. *"Look, Ali, just do it, OK?"*

"What's your hunch?" Ali asked, but Raven was obdurate.

"I can't tell you, not yet," she insisted. *"But see them as soon as you can. I'll be listening in."*

* * *

Wraith and Kez were in the gigantic foyer of the Countess's building, attempting to load the customized flitter which the Countess had provided them with. It was large enough to hold six people as well as the equipment they would need. But the loading was proving difficult as they were forced to work around Raven, who had already seated herself in the back of the vehicle and alternated between staring into space and suddenly turning to glare at them when they inadvertently interrupted her. Wraith was also trying to keep a look out for the back-up the Countess had arranged for them. She had agreed to provide them with three of her own guards, although the price had been high, but had only said that they would be available shortly.

Wraith was keen to get moving. He wanted to break into the laboratory as soon as possible, ending the anxiety he felt for Ali as well as Rachel. But Raven, despite her suggestion that they get into position, had refused to provide him with any progress reports on her connection with Ali. He loaded the last case of munitions into the back of the flitter, stacking it carefully so it wouldn't come loose when they took off. Raven was drumming her fingers impatiently on another case, no longer locked into her transceiver link. When he had finished checking the gear, he crossed to sit opposite her.

"How's it going?" he asked.

"It's difficult to keep the link without access to the net," she told him. "Where's Kez?"

"Just outside," he replied. "Do you need him?"

"Not yet." Raven was frowning. "But he'll have to

pilot the flitter, unless one of the people you've hired can. If there's an emergency I might not be able to and you certainly can't."

Wraith ignored the aspersion.

"What has Ali said?" he asked. "Has she found Rachel?"

"Not yet." Raven gave him an odd look. "Don't ask me anything more, Wraith. I'm trying to think."

Wraith gave up the attempt to get anything out of Raven and left the flitter. Kez was outside, looking almost ready to run. In front of him stood three men, all in blue and gold gang colors, looking at him rather contemptuously. As Wraith appeared, the tallest turned to look at him.

"You're Wraith?" he asked belligerently.

"Yes," Wraith said coolly, adopting a confident stance; he could sense that this was going to be difficult.

"Melek," the ganger told him, then gestured to his two companions. "They're Finn and Jeeva." Finn only jerked his head at Wraith, but Jeeva took his hand in a firm grip. Wraith took a moment to consider his new companions. They were dressed much as the Countess's other guards, but gang motifs glared from their militaristic clothing and all three had braided hair dyed a dark blue and strung with metallic beads.

"This should be a simple retrieval operation," Wraith said, watching the gangers closely for any negative reaction. "But the place we're going up against will probably have some heavy security."

"The Countess said you're breaking into a government lab," Melek said. "No matter what kind of weaponry you're packing, four of us won't be enough people for that kind of op. The security will be too heavy." He paused for a moment before adding: "But I can bring some more people in . . ."

"No." Wraith cut him off and saw Melek's immediate glare echoed by his companions. He couldn't back down; the last thing he wanted was to have his operation taken over by gangers, but he didn't want to antagonize the people he would have to work with either. While he was considering his next move, Kez provided a distraction.

"What about me?" he demanded. "I'll be there too."

"Keep out of this, kid," Melek drawled dismissively, but Finn was more vocal.

"Stick to what you know," he sneered, looking Kez over deliberately. "*You* couldn't use our kind of weaponry." He grinned and Kez flushed angrily, his fists clenching.

"Leave it, Kez," Wraith warned, not wanting to get into a confrontation on this subject. In all honesty, he had his own doubts about Kez's presence. He trusted the boy, but he had no experience at this kind of operation, and he couldn't blame the gangers for considering him a liability.

Unfortunately Kez looked angry enough to press the issue and Wraith tried to change tack by switching back to the original discussion.

"Bringing more people in would be a mistake," he said swiftly. "I don't plan to launch a full-scale attack on the place. It'd take an army to succeed that way. I

want to make a low-level run, compromising the
outer perimeter of security. Once we're in we'll hack
into the security system to nullify any additional
threat."

"You're taking a risk," Melek said dubiously. "It'd
take an *electric* hacker to break into a strange system
and screw with it before we're burned by security."

"Raven can do it," Wraith assured them, but Finn
was already shaking his head.

"No way we should run with this, till we've seen
what he's got, Mel," he said brusquely. "I'm not getting flatlined because his hacker screwed up, and we
couldn't pull out in time."

"I'll go with that," the other ganger added and
Melek turned to Wraith with a mocking smile.

"You heard my brothers," he challenged. "We
want to see what your hacker's got before we go
with you."

"That wasn't the deal," Wraith objected.

"It is now," Melek told him, and waited.

The sound of raised voices distracted Raven; it
was a niggling itch in the back of her head that dis-
rupted her already fragile connection with Ali's
transceiver. Annoyed at the reminder that her abilities were not as far-ranging as she might wish, she
abandoned the link and got to her feet, emerging
from the flitter just in time to hear Melek declare the
change in plans.

She noticed with satisfaction that Kez blanched as
she jumped down from the vehicle to join the group.
She was in a sufficiently bad mood to welcome an ar-

gument and it seemed that one was on the cards. Ignoring the presence of the strangers she spoke directly to Wraith.

"How long are we going to hang about here?" she demanded. "I want us to be in position by 1900 this evening. Let's get going."

"We may have a problem here, Raven . . ." Wraith began slowly, but was interrupted.

"This is your hacker?" Melek demanded incredulously, turning to look Raven over carefully. Raven returned the look, stare for stare, and registered at the back of her mind that both Wraith and Kez took a step backward as the tension built. She was always ready for a confrontation. Wary of the fact that she had no reputation in England, she had prepared herself for this. The black-eyed stare that Ali had found so disconcerting was not an untried tactic, and it was one with a high success rate. Raven didn't just look at the ganger, she looked *through* him. And as her gaze washed over him like ice-cold water she filled it with everything she had discovered about him over the network. The gangers were hardly inconspicuous and all three had criminal records of impressive length; another conviction would be enough to get any of them a long custody sentence. But Raven had pulled out more data than that. She knew about their drug habits, their squats, she even knew about their families, and she held that knowledge in her eyes as she looked at them. She heard Finn and Jeeva mirror Wraith and Kez's retreat, stepping away from that stare. But she held Melek's gaze, pressing for that extra advantage, waiting for the right psychological moment.

Then it came, a brief flicker, and the ganger's gaze left hers, unable to hold it any longer. Raven allowed herself a slight smile before she spoke.

"I'm the hacker," she agreed. "And you need have *no* doubts about my abilities." She let the statement hang in the air, waiting for their response. Finn's came first, a muttered aside to Jeeva:

"Freakin' skitzo . . ."

But Melek was more controlled, knowing that he had to preserve his confidence or lose the respect of his subordinates.

"You're confident enough," he shrugged. "But that don't count for nothing when the Seccies are on your tail."

"I'm confident with reason," Raven said coldly. Then, having displayed enough ice to alarm them, she allowed herself to relax. "And I'm good enough to wipe you from the Seccie records . . ." She grinned at their widened eyes. "That's the pay-off," she added. "As well as the creds, I'll clean you off the system. Make you invisible."

She didn't wait for Melek's nod. Agreement was a foregone conclusion, the offer irresistible. As the gangers shook hands with Wraith to clinch the deal, she headed for the flitter's controls. Kez seated himself beside her in the front.

"You're not scared of anything, are you?" he said in a low voice. Raven glanced at him as she powered up the craft. She could have told him how she felt about where they were heading, the reasons why she didn't like to think about the laboratory where Ali was trapped. Her fingers flew over the computer unit that formed part of the control panel, her mind sinking into the technology as she renewed the link with Ali.

"No, I'm not," she lied.

Ali felt sick.

Luciel had been unwilling to show her the three surviving victims of the memory experiments but she had insisted, impelled by Raven's insistence that it was important for her to locate them. Now she believed that Luciel had been right and Raven wrong. These children would not be able to tell her anything about Rachel.

Tom had joined them as well, although he was as morose as ever. Ali suspected he had agreed to accompany them simply because she provided a diversion. But she was relieved that he had chosen to come. The three survivors were housed on another floor of the facility and it was obvious that Luciel became increasingly nervous the further away from his room he was. The elevator had two panels. One with option settings for three floors, the other covered with a metal plate with a key-lock rather than a computer-coded locking device. Tom had noticed her looking and shrugged.

"Access to the rest of the facility is restricted," he told her. "And they don't want to risk any of us getting computer access. That's why they use outdated recording methods most of the time. You've probably noticed that they take down test results on paper."

Ali had nodded, thinking silently that the computer room—that Raven had claimed existed—was probably on one of those restricted floors. The floor the elevator took them to was almost identical to the one they had left. The only real difference was the nature of the test-subjects. Almost all of them were confined to their beds, either because they were incapable of moving, or because they were held there by heavy restraints. Tom led them to the end of the first corridor and opened a door, walking with the minimum of movement and obviously self-conscious about the jerky machine-enhanced reactions of his body.

Once inside both Luciel and Ali had paused, frozen in place as they looked at the figure lying on the bed. Tom regarded them with a curious satisfaction at their reaction. He had been right when he spoke of Mikhail being covered in more machinery than him. The boy on the bed lay in the midst of a tangle of cables and medical equipment. He was naked, except for a pair of shorts, and Ali could see that the machinery extended further. Metal seemed to have been welded to his skin, giving him an inhuman appearance. And from the flesh that survived, stretched tight over the bones of the skeletal figure, came the unmistakable stench of corruption. The boy was literally rotting away. As she stared in fascinated horror, her eyes met Mikhail's and she realized with shock that his expression was not vacant. Within that living corpse, he was still, against all reason, horribly aware.

Her stomach heaved and she turned quickly, fumbling for the door and escaping into the corridor. Taking deep breaths she sank to the floor, half retching, half sobbing. As her body shook in paroxysms of fear she heard a quiet voice buzz in her ear.

"What happened?"

She couldn't speak as she continued to gasp for breath and Raven's voice took on an edge of what might have been alarm as she continued:

"Ali, your heart rate's gone right up—you're going into shock. Get a hold of yourself and tell me what happened."

"Raven." Ali bent her head and murmured the words into her folded arms. "I saw . . . I saw one of the test-subjects for the memory experiments . . . It was, it was so horrible . . ." She cut herself off abruptly as Tom and Luciel emerged from the room. Luciel bent to help her to her feet.

"Are you OK?" he asked with concern.

"I think so," she said shakily.

"Then you want to go on?" Tom asked and grimaced a little in response to her nod. "It won't do any good," he said. "We asked Mikhail about your friend. He didn't tell us anything. He doesn't speak anymore."

"This is pointless, Ali." Luciel looked distressed. "The other two won't be able to tell us anything either. Mikhail won't talk, Esther can't, and Revenge is incomprehensible."

Ali hesitated and heard Raven speak softly into her ear:

"Say you want to go on."

She sighed, wondering how the others would react if she told them she heard voices in her head telling her to continue. Rejecting the impulse she said only:

"I want to see them." Tom and Luciel exchanged glances, but set off again in search of the next patient.

If the gangers hadn't known that Raven was a Hex when they got into the flitter, they must certainly know by now. Wraith frowned when he realized that Raven was making no attempt to disguise her abilities. But he rationalized that the Countess had assured him they would be discreet, and that he would be trusting these people with their lives anyway. However, Raven's use of her Hex abilities made him uncomfortable. Her preference for working in seclusion meant that he had not exactly been aware of what her connection with computers entailed.

Now he found it slightly alarming to see her sitting in the pilot's seat, one hand resting lightly on the controls, her eyes defocused. The flitter weaved past the buildings at high speed, avoiding the rest of the aerial traffic, but the sight of Raven's blank eyes made him tight with tension. The gangers seemed to be similarly affected, if the care with which they had fastened themselves into the vehicle was any indication. The only person who seemed at ease was Kez, who hadn't fastened his own belt, and was grinning with every evidence of enjoyment at the high speeds the flitter was attaining. His absence of alarm seemed to increase his status in the eyes of the gangers. Wraith leaned forward with a deliberate ease to speak to Raven.

"Can you hear me?" he asked.

"Naturally," she replied somewhat caustically. "But there's a limit to how many things I can do at once. I'm not really in the mood for conversation."

"Are you in contact with Ali?" Wraith said, ignoring her tone.

"Yes."

"If you want to concentrate on your link with her, you needn't pilot as well," Wraith suggested.

"I think I can handle it," Raven said, a shade of amusement in her voice, although her eyes remained blank. "If there's a problem I'll hand over to Kez."

"Very well," Wraith agreed, reflecting to himself that, given Kez's propensity for speeding, the exchange would hardly make much difference. As he sat back he caught Melek's gaze and the ganger gave an almost rueful shrug. Wraith acknowledged it with the barest flicker of his eyes, but he sensed the mood in the flitter become less antagonistic.

The second of the patients was no more communicative than the first. But Ali found herself more able to handle Esther's vacuity than Mikhail's consciousness. The girl was one of the oldest patients. According to Tom she had been in her late teens when admitted and was now in her early twenties. He had added, almost without interest, that test-subjects rarely survived that long. Ali wondered if Esther's state could be called surviving. Her mind had been damaged by the experiments, leaving her with the mental abilities of a small child. She smiled lopsidedly at a point somewhere behind their heads as Luciel questioned her, and it was obvious to Ali that there was no way she would be telling them anything about Rachel. Raven obviously concurred. After only a few minutes of questioning Esther, her voice came over the comlink again.

"We're accomplishing nothing here."

Ali tried to conceal her frustration. The presence of the others meant that she couldn't point out to Raven that this had been a useless exercise from the beginning. Instead she turned to Luciel.

"Can you show me the third test-subject?" she asked.

"Revenge?" Luciel sighed. "I guess so. I suppose you won't be satisfied until we do."

"Come on then," Tom said gruffly, heading for the door. "Let's get this charade over with."

He led the way down the corridor and through three more sets of doors until he halted before a shut door. He moved to open it and then paused, the hum of his machinery dropping to a low purr as he cautioned Ali:

"Revenge is under permanent restraint because she often becomes violent. If she starts acting up, we had better get out of here. I don't want *them* to turn up and start asking us what we're doing here."

"OK," Ali agreed and Luciel added his assent, obviously equally unwilling to come into contact with the scientists. Tom turned back to the door and pushed it open.

A girl was lying on the bed, metal cuffs holding her wrists to the sides of the bed and a heavy over-blanket buckled tightly over her so she couldn't move her body. She had been sitting as far up the bed as the restraints allowed, leaning back against the pillows. But as the door opened her head snapped round and she fixed them with a piercing stare. She looked more like an old woman than a child. Her features were gaunt and her eyes sunken. Her hands clutched the sides of the bed like claws and her wrists were flecked with blood, lacerated by the cuffs. Her hair would have been waist length if it was brushed, but instead it was matted around her head in a dirty mess. Her skin was grimy, and there was dried blood from the scratches on her face and bruises on her neck. In a facility where everything else was clinically sanitized she seemed incongruous. Looking at her injuries Ali felt convinced they were self-inflicted.

Tom approached the bed hesitantly and the girl focused on him with a fearful intensity, her lips drawing back to show her teeth in an animal snarl. Luciel looked nervous and Ali found herself holding her breath as Tom spoke.

"Revenge?" he said soothingly. "It's Tom . . . will you talk to me?"

There was a growl. If the girl had been an animal she would have flattened her ears; as it was she flinched back, looking as if she would bite if Tom came any closer. Ali jumped when a human voice rasped from Revenge's torn mouth.

"You are poisoned," she hissed. "Infected. Get away from me!" Her voice rose to a scream and both Tom and Luciel retreated. Luciel glanced sideways at Ali.

"You wanted to talk to her," he said. "Good luck."

She wet her lips nervously and prepared to speak, wondering what it was Raven expected of her. But before she could say anything a voice spoke in her ear.

"*Relax, Ali,*" Raven told her. "*Repeat exactly what I say.*" Ali couldn't respond, but Raven took her assent as read and began softly: "*Ask her name.*"

"What's your name?" Ali said obediently and the cadaverous face turned to regard her.

"I am Revenge," she said, looking through Ali in a way that was eerily familiar.

"Is that a name or a threat?" Raven's voice was chilling.

"Uh . . . is that a name or a threat?" Ali asked uncomfortably.

"It's what I am," Revenge whispered, leaning forward ominously. Ali resisted the urge to flinch back as she added: "There is nothing else . . ." Her bloodied lips parted in a terrible smile, and Ali found herself staring into the eyes of insanity.

Raven's attention was almost entirely concentrated on the link. Lacking Ali's physical presence, she was blind to what the other girl saw. But the words that came through the link resounded in her ears. She perceived the flow of a thousand streams of data as she searched databases all over Europe, concentrating on one word:

> revenge <

> revenge <

> revenge <

The test-subjects in the memory experiments had been linked up to a computer database. Which one? What had it contained? Raven was hardly conscious of Ali transmitting her words as she spoke directly to the shattered figure on the bed.

"Who are you?"

There was no answer, but the transmitter reported a rise in Ali's heart rate. And then Raven heard the girl's voice:

"You speak out of the dark . . ."

She froze. It was impossible for the girl to know that she was speaking through Ali. Impossible, but her words suggested that, somehow, she *did* know. Raven felt the pressure of that darkness, fought against the urge to throw off her contact with the computer network, and just then one of the myriad tendrils of her awareness caught hold of a piece of information and brought it to her consciousness.

> re·venge {ri'ven(d)$_3$} I. v/t. 1. *et,. a. j-n* rächen ([*up*]*on* an *dat.*): *to ~ o.s. for s.th.* sich für et. rachen; *to be ~d* a) gerächt sein *od.* werden, b) sich rächen; 2. sich rächen für, vergelten (*upon, on* an *dat.*); II. *s.* 3. Rache *f:* . . .<

The association that had lodged somewhere in Raven's eidetic memory had been located. She focused on the dictionary entry for a heartbeat, an eon in the virtual time of the network. Whatever twisted logic had led the girl through the Germanic association of her name to a deadly statement of intent was lost now. But from a chain of half-formed clues Raven had unraveled the truth. She directed a new message to Ali's comlink and as she spoke she acknowledged the reality of what she had discovered.

"Hello, Rachel."

9

The Mortal Sword

"Rachel?" Ali exclaimed. Luciel and Tom turned to stare at her, but before they could say a word they were interrupted by a raw scream. Revenge had lunged for Ali, fighting to escape the cuffs, her body thrashing with effort.

"Raven! Raven, where are you?" she screamed. The two boys looked baffled. But Ali knew that this was the most rational thing Revenge had said so far.

"We'd better go," Tom urged and Ali looked from him to Revenge, uncertain of what to do.

"Ali, speak to her," Raven ordered. *"Repeat after me . . ."*

Ali listened, memorizing Raven's words. Grabbing Revenge's arms she held her down on the bed and lowered her voice to repeat what she had been told:

"Be still . . . Raven comes . . . wait for her . . ."

"Yes," Revenge hissed, her eyes burning with anticipation. "Tell her, soon . . . she must come soon, or it will be too late."

Raven blinked. The flitter had reached the edges of London. The towering skyscrapers were thinning out. The concrete jungle continued in a line across the countryside, a tangle of roads curving on top of and around each other, bordered by the towering skyrises. Raven guided the flitter out over the highway, careful not to deviate from her course into the no-fly zone over the agricultural lands. As she did so, she slowly drew her mind back from the computer connection, severing both it and the link with Ali.

She took a breath slowly. She wasn't certain of why she was unwilling to speak. But she doubted that her reticence came from anything so basic as a consideration for Wraith. The fact that Rachel was still alive bound them to their purpose, impelled them to break into the laboratory, but the things that Ali had discovered there made Raven extremely unwilling to move any nearer the reach of the CPS. Her right hand clenched into a fist on the controls and the flitter leaped forward with a lurch, shifting into a higher speed. She refused to accept the fear that threatened to control her. Instead she savored the roar of the wind rushing past them and said without emotion:

"We've found Rachel."

"You have?" Wraith sounded tense and Raven turned to meet his eyes. "Is she . . . How is she?" he asked, trying to preserve his mask of control.

"Her mind has been severely affected by the testing," Raven said dispassionately. "But she appears to retain some measure of sanity."

"Some measure of sanity?" Wraith looked frozen and Raven heard Kez's soft gasp of distress. She felt distanced from both of them, identifying herself with the three disinterested gangers in the back of the flitter rather than with her anxious brother.

"Be thankful she's not brain-dead or flatlined," she stated. "Her condition is better than I thought it would be."

Kez tried to stretch his cramped muscles and frowned. Large as the flitter was, the passenger seat was not the most comfortable place he'd been, especially after the long flight. The gangers and Wraith had room in the back to stretch out, even with the packing cases. But, cramped as he was, Kez hesitated to join them. Melek had been antagonistic to his presence on the operation and he didn't want to provoke the gangers into making their disapproval more immediately felt. As it was he tried to make himself comfortable in his seat and alternated between dozing and looking out of the window.

The latter of these two alternatives was easier to accomplish. Raven had been obliged to keep below the speed limit, since they didn't want to attract the attention of the Seccies with a cargo of armaments, and had therefore increased the volume of her rock music to painful levels. Kez suspected that this was also a function of her wish to avoid conversation. Wraith was clearly concerned about Rachel's condition and Raven just as obviously wanted to avoid the issue. However, every now and then the music paused as Raven changed disks and Kez took advantage of one of these breaks to engage her attention.

"You're still not piloting manually?"

"As you see." Raven shrugged. Her seat was tilted back and her legs stretched out on top of the bank of controls, only one hand resting lightly on a set of controls to her left.

"What would happen if you fell asleep?"

"I'm not certain," Raven said slowly, and then grinned. "Want to find out?"

"I don't think so." Kez shook his head but he was smiling as well. Raven's good humor relieved a little of his anxiety about what they were doing. "Are you tired, though? If you are I can take over." He made the suggestion a little hesitantly, but Raven didn't seem annoyed by it. She shrugged again.

"I'm OK," she said. "There's not much point in changing places now—we're almost there."

"We are?"

"Look outside," Raven suggested, and Kez turned to the window.

It was almost dusk and it was hard for him to make anything out in the dim half-light. Raven seemed to have left the main roadway, and the lights of the buildings that surrounded it were nowhere to be seen; gone also were the running lights of other flitters. But Raven had kept their own lights on and Kez could catch glimpses of the dark countryside, a town or city in the distance lighting up the sky, and below them the black ribbon of a minor road and the streaks of light as skimmers sped by. Up ahead were the darker masses of hills and Raven gestured toward them.

"That's where the lab is. But, according to the transport database, everything on either side of this road is restricted airspace."

"Isn't there an approach road?" Wraith asked.

"We'd hardly use it if there was," Raven pointed out. "But no, there's nothing indicated." She considered. "I expect there is one though, and it'll be in the government databases so their operatives can reach the lab."

"Pull that database," Wraith told her. "We don't want to use that road, but we don't want to stumble across it by accident either."

"Better cut the running lights," Melek added. "Since this is a covert op, best not to get seen."

"I can't cut them while we're still over the main roadway," Raven pointed out, her eyes already defocusing as she connected to the network. "If a Seccie monitor caught us flying without lights they'd order us to halt. But I'll swing off the road in about thirty minutes and cut the lights then. If anyone does catch us entering restricted airspace, we'll send a com message saying we had technical problems."

"A power loss?" Kez suggested. "That would explain why you'd cut the lights."

"With any luck the eventuality won't come up," Wraith said. "Any luck with that road, Raven?"

"Found it," she stated. "There's an exit from the main roadway. Blink and you'd miss it. Then there's about a kilometer from the turn-off to the outer perimeter of the facility."

"Break off from the road before you reach it," Wraith ordered. "Then bring the flitter down behind trees or something. I don't want us to make the run on the lab until later tonight. We can catch a couple of hours sleep while we're waiting."

Ali lay flat on her back on the bed trying to stay calm. The revelation that Rachel was Revenge had shocked her. She was still trying to come to terms with its significance. The girl's grip on sanity seemed so tenuous that she doubted if even Raven could understand her. But Raven had seemed to know the right things to say to calm her sister down, without arousing Tom and Luciel's suspicions.

Ali sighed. The thought of the two boys was what troubled her most. She was surprised at how confident she was of Raven and Wraith's ability to rescue her. Her only doubts concerned what that escape would mean. She and Revenge were not the only prisoners in the facility. The idea of leaving the others trapped in the lab while she saved her own skin was rapidly becoming unpalatable. Ali could hardly imagine that Raven would take well to her altruistic impulse, but she had to try.

She rolled over to bury her head in the pillow and whispered almost under her breath:

"Raven. Raven, are you there? I have to talk to you." There was no reply. Ali waited, then repeated herself, but still there was nothing. She felt icy fingers grip her heart and had to force herself not to panic. Raven had said that the link was unbreakable. They'd been steadily in contact for hours with no mention of danger. Nothing could have gone wrong. She paused in her rapid calculations as a new thought hit her. It was only logical really. She could hardly be surprised if Raven proved herself human and succumbed to a human weakness like falling asleep. But this was hardly the best time. She sat up, frowning. Then she blinked in surprise at the sight of a face peering through the glass panel on the door.

It was Luciel. He pushed the door open hesitantly, revealing Tom standing behind him.

"Can I come in?" he asked.

"We need to talk to you," Tom added.

"OK," Ali agreed, feeling uneasy. She couldn't help the thought that all three of them were under a death sentence that at present only she had a chance of escaping. "What about?"

"You're going to try to escape," Tom said flatly and Ali started. Luciel was already nodding agreement.

"You're here for Revenge," he said softly. "I don't know why, but I'm sure that's it."

"Are you even a Hex at all?" Tom demanded, although he kept his voice low.

"I am a Hex," Ali admitted, her mind racing as she tried to think of a way to evade the rest of the questions. Where was Raven when she needed her? But the comlink was silent and she had to make the decision of what to tell them on her own. The choice was surprisingly easy. "You're right," she said. "I am going to break out."

"You don't have a hope in hell," Tom said, shaking his head. "There's no *way* you'll manage that."

"She got in, didn't she?" Luciel said. "If she could get in, and find Revenge, she must have a way to get out."

"I'll have help," Ali said softly. "I'm not here on my own. There's a group of people, gangers, who'll be helping me."

"You mean you and Revenge," Tom corrected.

"Yes," Ali nodded.

"Why?" Luciel looked baffled. "Why Revenge? She's brain-fried. What good would she do you?"

"Her brother's one of the gangers," Ali told him. "And her sister . . ." She broke off abruptly, deciding that it would be a bad idea to mention Raven. She'd probably annoy the other girl enough when Raven found out Ali had told them about the rest of the team, without exacerbating that. Ali knew Raven well enough to realize that she wouldn't take kindly to a betrayal of her identity.

But even without mentioning Raven, Ali was worried that she'd gone too far. They were in a high-security facility and a single word to a scientist would be enough to stop the retrieval before it started. Wraith had kept his team small deliberately, planning to use surprise as his primary weapon. If Ali gave away that element of surprise, the team really wouldn't have a chance.

"You mustn't say a word," she cautioned hurriedly. "Please?"

Tom and Luciel looked at each other. Luciel was the first to speak.

"We won't say anything, Ali," he said. "But if you're really escaping . . ."

"We're coming with you," Tom finished. "And so is everyone else kept prisoner here. You won't be going alone."

Kez woke with a start as someone shook him. He opened his eyes blearily to see a ghost-like shadow standing over him. Wraith's gray eyes stared at him, his mop of white hair blowing out around his face.

"Time for an equipment check," he said curtly and Kez nodded, yawning as he sat up. "I need you to explain the functions of those devices of Raven's," Wraith continued.

"Why can't she do it?" Kez protested, glancing over to where the three gangers sat against the side of the flitter. They looked as if they'd been awake for some time already.

"She's still asleep," Wraith told him. "I don't want to wake her until I have to. We'll be needing her tonight."

Kez wondered if that meant *he* wasn't needed. But the fact that Wraith had asked for his assistance suggested he wasn't entirely useless. He got to his feet, pushing away the coat that he'd been sleeping under, and wandered over to the flitter. Raven was stretched out over the front two seats. She looked exhausted, dark shadows under her eyes. He sighed. The success or failure of this operation was essentially resting on Raven. But although they had to put their trust in her she refused to do the same for them. She pushed herself to the limits of endurance rather than rely on anyone but herself.

A hand dropped onto his shoulder, making him

jump, and he turned to see one of the gangers standing behind him. It was Jeeva and he was grinning, somewhat to Kez's relief.

"Hey, kid. Does he know you're cruising his sister?" He jerked his head at the flitter. Wraith and the two other gangers were already checking through the equipment.

"I'm not cruising her," Kez objected, and then shrugged. "And even if I was it wouldn't make any difference. Raven's only interested in one person."

"Herself, right?" Jeeva slapped Kez's shoulder and gave him a twisted smile. "So, forget about her, kid. Don't waste the effort on the ice queen. C'mon, let's go."

"Yeah, OK." Kez fell into step with Jeeva, realizing to his own amazement that he had had a conversation with a ganger without getting flatlined.

Wraith only listened with half an ear to Kez's explanation of the explosive charges, concentrating on checking the artillery he would be taking with him. All three gangers had a combat rifle slung over one shoulder and the ammunition for it, as well as handguns hanging from their belts. Wraith had chosen more specialized weaponry, but like the gangers he was wearing extensive body armor. He glanced over at Kez, frowning slightly. The boy was demonstrating how to activate the frequency oscillator which would cause Raven's devices to explode within five seconds. The boy was dressed simply and his only weapon was the laser pistol that hung from his belt.

Wraith wondered if it was too late to forbid Kez to come with them. He seemed more likely to be a liability to the gangers than any assistance. He glanced toward the front of the flitter where Raven was still asleep. Their plan of action called for Kez to act as her cover. If Wraith pulled him off the mission it would affect her the most. He leaned over the back of the seats and looked at Raven. She must be exhausted to sleep so long and he had almost decided not to wake her when she spoke:

"What is it, Wraith?" she asked, her eyes still shut.

"Kez," he said quietly, too low for the others to hear him. "He doesn't have the experience for something like this."

"That didn't seem to worry you too much before." Raven opened her eyes and considered him. "And it's not as if we had a great many options. We needed to keep the team small, and Kez is a streetkid. He can take care of himself."

"What if he can't?" Wraith asked. "We need you to get into that computer system, Raven. If something happens to Kez you won't have any back-up, and the rest of us will be relying on you alone."

"I'll get into the system," Raven assured him. "With or without Kez." She sat up and stretched, sighing a little. "Wraith, we've gone over this enough times before. If we change our plans now we'll only be endangering ourselves."

Wraith studied his sister for a few more seconds, but he didn't contradict her. The strategy she was advocating had been his own and he agreed with it. But everything seemed so much colder when it came from

Raven. Eventually he acknowledged what she had said with a curt nod. "You'd better get ready," he told her. "We should be ready to leave within half an hour."

The flitter approached the perimeter of the facility, only just above ground level. Raven had relinquished the pilot's seat to Kez, who was concentrating determinedly on the difficulties of the course Wraith had dictated. They could see the gray shape of the laboratory buildings in the distance, beyond the electric fencing. Melek was studying this intently as Kez landed the flitter.

"That's not very sophisticated security for a government facility," he said suspiciously.

"It doesn't need a lot of security," Wraith pointed out. "Almost no one knows it exists, and even if they did, popular feeling is so against Hexes that there's little danger of any one trying to rescue them from the scientists."

"It's not as innocent as it looks," Raven said quietly. "There are motion sensors and vidcams focused on that fence."

"How do you know?" Kez asked and Raven gestured to the computer console on the flitter.

"The Countess knew what she was doing when she rigged out this thing," she told him. "But it hasn't been able to detect anything behind the immediate vicinity of the fence. As soon as I get into that security system we'll be OK, but until then it'll be hard going."

"Can those motion sensors detect us from here?" Wraith asked and Raven shook her head.

"Not until we're five meters from the fence."

"Right." Wraith turned to the rest of the team. "Don't let those sensors pick you up. We'll have to shoot them out, simultaneously. When they're out of the way we can get through the fence. Stay in contact"—he gestured to the com unit round his wrist—"and try to keep things quiet. We want to get in, pick up Ali and Rachel and get out again. Nothing else. While my group looks for the girls, Raven will hack into the computers and neutralize the security system. Let's make this as quick and as clean as we can. Is that clear?"

"We scan," Melek told him. "Stay chill, brothers." He nodded to Kez, as an afterthought. "Good luck, kid."

"Raven," Wraith said. "Are you set?"

"Everything's under control," she told him, already unlocking the doors of the flitter.

"Then let's go."

The group approached the fence cautiously as Raven pointed out the sensors that would have to be neutralized. Once she had identified them all, Wraith positioned Kez and the gangers ready to shoot them down. With each of them targeted on a sensor, there were still two vidcams to be put out of action and he intended that he and Raven should deal with those. However, it was not until he'd unholstered his gun that Raven reached under her long coat to produce one of her own. It didn't look that different from a long-barreled pistol. But instead of loading it, Raven tapped a key sequence across a panel on the butt of the pistol and it emitted a low hum.

"What is that?" Wraith asked curiously and Raven shrugged a shoulder.

"Electrical energy," she told him. "I designed it. There are certain advantages to it." As she finished speaking she leveled the pistol at one of the vidcams, then turned to look at Wraith expectantly. He turned to the other, trying to ignore the fact that Raven had sighted on her target in under a second, concentrating on his own. He kept his eyes on it as he asked:

"Ready?" There was a low murmur of assent and Wraith continued. "Fire on three. One ... two ... three!"

There was a soft roar, then a flash of sparks as the sensors and vidcams exploded on cue. Wraith checked them instinctively. Apparently everyone on the team had made their targets. Melek and Finn were already moving in to attack the wire of the fence, using lasers to cut through a section without being electrocuted.

"Security will have been alerted as soon as those sensors stopped transmitting," Raven reminded them. "We've got to reach the lab building before they catch up with us."

"OK, get going," Wraith ordered as the section of fence collapsed, sprinting for the building. The gangers were immediately behind him, and Raven and Kez brought up the rear.

It was then that Raven heard a voice in her ears, coming through the comlink that she'd left active before falling asleep.

"Raven, can you hear me?"

"Now is not the time, Ali," she hissed as she ran, keeping her voice low.

"*I need to talk to you,*" Ali insisted.

"Are you in danger?" Raven demanded.

"*No, but . . .*"

"Then, forget it, Ali! We'll be with you soon enough!" Raven snapped and cut contact. The distraction had left her several paces behind Kez and she speeded up, trying to move faster over the uneven ground.

Wraith had the plans in mind as he approached the lab. However much the facility might have changed on the inside it appeared that the layout on the outside hadn't altered substantially. Over to the right he could see lights and unhesitatingly identified them as belonging to the approach road and the main entrance of the lab. But he led his team to the left and what had been marked on the plans as a service entrance.

They were still two hundred meters away from the door when there was a sudden glare of lights and the sound of an alarm. Wraith swore under his breath and dropped to the ground, waving the others to join him. The gangers were with him immediately and Kez only a second after them. Raven raced up a moment later, her black coat flapping out behind her as she threw herself beside them. For a while there seemed to be no security reaction other than the siren and searchlights sweeping over the ground, and Melek grabbed Wraith's arm.

"Those lights are going to catch up to us real soon," he warned.

"I know. Stay chill," Wraith told him. He was

scanning the area carefully, looking for any signs of response, but it was Kez who noticed it first.

"Wraith! Over there," he said urgently.

Three uniformed security personnel were approaching from the direction of the main entrance, carrying rifles. Melek reached for his gun but Wraith pushed his hand away.

"Not yet," he cautioned. "Wait." Melek halted his motion, but Finn was not as circumspect. Either he hadn't heard Wraith's warning or he deliberately chose to disregard it. His combat rifle roared and one of the guards fell. The other two threw themselves out of the line of fire and Raven hissed in annoyance.

"That's torn it," she exclaimed.

"Melek, Finn, deal with those two. Try and get them out of the way before they can call for back-up."

"Some chance," Raven said under her breath but Wraith ignored it.

"Raven, you're with me," he ordered. "Jeeva, Kez, cover us." He leaped to his feet and headed for the service entrance, Raven following close behind. This time his instructions were apparently obeyed. Melek and Finn had opened fire on the guards behind them and, as he and Raven were halfway to the door, he heard more gunfire begin. He looked left in time to see two more guards seeking cover from Jeeva and Kez's fire. Then they had reached the door and there was no time for him to worry about what was happening. He had to rely on his team's ability to do their job. Raven was already examining the door.

"It's physically locked from the inside," she told him. "We'll have to blast it open."

"How many?" Wraith asked, grabbing two of the explosive charges from the bag he had slung over one shoulder.

"Not those." Raven shook her head. "We wouldn't have enough time to trigger enough of them. Give me a moment."

She rummaged in the deep pockets of her coat, producing what looked like a net. The fire-fight went on behind them as Raven unrolled the object, revealing it to be an electronic mesh of circuitry and explosives, and attached it to the door.

"Come on," she told Wraith. "Follow me." They were about ten meters from the door when she turned back and fired her pistol at the mesh. Electricity crackled over it in a glowing net before Raven pushed her brother to the ground. Seconds later the door exploded behind them. As it did so Jeeva and Kez ran toward them. Wraith stood, dragging Raven up with him, and they all headed for the door.

"We got the two who were shooting at you just now," Jeeva told Wraith as they made it inside. Wraith nodded at him and turned on his com unit, keying it to Melek's signal.

"Wraith here," he said. "What's happening?"

"*We'll be done here in a moment, brother.*" The ganger's voice came from the unit, overlaid with the sound of heavy fire. "*You get that door open?*"

"It's down," Wraith told him. "We're going in."

Ali lay in bed, wide awake. Two of the scientists had patrolled the corridors in the evening, making certain that all the test-subjects were restricted to

their own rooms. Luciel and Tom had been reluctant to leave, but they were better acquainted with the rules of the lab than she was and didn't want to risk arousing the scientists' suspicions. Ali had told them to be ready for anything.

She wore her white overalls in bed, knowing that she'd need to act at a moment's notice. But she had no idea of what acting would entail. Somewhere outside, the gangers were breaking into the laboratory, in danger of their lives, and she was stuck in a room unable to do anything. She felt useless and more than that, helpless. Her life was dependent on Wraith and Raven's ability to rescue her.

A dark shape moved by the door and Ali caught her breath in alarm. Then there was a familiar hum of machinery and she recognized Tom. Luciel wasn't far behind him as they slipped into the room together.

"What's going on?" Ali whispered, climbing from under the covers.

"That's for us to ask you," Tom pointed out. "You said your team would be breaking in tonight. Where are they?"

"I don't know," Ali admitted. "But they *are* on their way in. I tried to contact Raven, to tell her about . . . about what we discussed and she cut me off. I think things are getting serious outside."

"Wait!" Luciel looked stunned. "You can contact them?"

"Only Raven," Ali admitted, wondering when she would hear the last of this. "And we're not in contact right now."

"But something's happening, right?" Tom said. "What are we going to do if your gangers don't know that we're coming with you?"

"I'll tell them," Ali promised. "But I can't do it while they're breaking in. If I distract them I'd be endangering us as well as them. Besides . . ." she hesitated, "I don't think we can take everyone with us."

"What?" Tom looked angry, but Luciel's eyes were understanding.

"There are just too many people, Tom," he said softly. "Not enough of them are mobile. We'd never get out."

"We can only take those who can walk by themselves," Ali said as decisively as she could. "We can't do anything more."

10

Striding the Blast

Melek and Finn raced through the door, almost cannoning into Kez and panting for breath.

"We got them," Melek gasped. "But there are more coming!"

"We need to find that control center," Wraith told them. "Find a computer terminal so Raven can locate it." He was already moving, gesturing for Melek to join him. "Finn and Jeeva, bring up the rear. Raven, whatever you do, don't get yourself shot." He heard Raven make a derisive noise behind him, but she seemed to be keeping up.

They thundered down the corridor, turning a corner just in time to avoid gunfire from behind. They were passing rooms which might contain an access terminal but they just couldn't risk the time to search. Another corner loomed and Wraith skidded around it. Finn and Jeeva were firing behind; presumably the guards were getting closer. Ahead of them he could see an elevator, which must lead to the part of the facility which was underground, and the corridor branched in two directions. He was trying to decide which to take when the elevator doors slid open. A scientist in a white lab coat stared at them in horror and tried to close the doors, but Melek forestalled her. He forced them open, pulling the woman out and knocking her unconscious with a swift blow.

"Keep the guards back!" Wraith called to the other two gangers, who stayed at the turn of the corridor, firing a fusillade of shots. Kez grabbed some of his stock of explosives and switched them to explode before lobbing them down the corridor one by one. The resultant explosion was loud enough to make Wraith wince, but it seemed to be successful as Jeeva called to him that there was no one else in pursuit.

Wraith didn't doubt that more guards were on the way but it seemed that there was a problem with the elevator.

"What's wrong?" he demanded as Melek cursed.

"The panel's locked down," the ganger told him.

"Raven?" Wraith asked, but she shook her head. "It's a physical lock. I can't fuse it." However, she did produce a small tool and set to work on the panel.

"What's holding us up?" Finn demanded as he and Jeeva reached the others.

"The elevator controls are locked," Wraith told him and Raven looked up.

"Wraith, try to find another way down," she told him. "There must be emergency stairs. Try to find where they're holding the test-subjects." Wraith hesitated for only a second then he nodded quickly.

"Jeeva, Kez, stay with her," he ordered and headed down the corridor with the other two gangers.

Kez looked around nervously, holding the elevator doors open so Raven could work on the panel. Jeeva was watching the corridor warily, holding his gun ready in case more guards should turn up. Suddenly Raven gave a grunt of satisfaction and the panel clattered to the floor of the lift.

"Get in," she told them. "We've got to go now!" Kez and Jeeva didn't need any more persuasion; in seconds they were in the elevator.

"Which floor?" Kez asked and Raven frowned.

"We'll try this one first," she said, pressing the appropriate button as the doors slid shut. "On the original plans this floor was used for administration —there should be terminals there, even if the control room isn't."

The ride took less than a minute, and as the elevator slowed both Raven and Jeeva readied their weapons.

"Get back," Jeeva warned him and Kez flattened himself against the right-hand wall of the car next to the ganger. Raven had already moved to the other side. As the doors slid open bullets clanged off the back wall and Raven and Jeeva opened fire simultaneously.

"Explosive!" Raven hissed and Kez quickly switched the one he held to detonate, counted to four, and threw it through the doors. A second later it exploded and there were shouts of alarm. Jeeva quickly leaned out of the elevator and fired several rapid shots. Then he turned to nod at them.

"Three dead," he said. "We'd better get going."

"There must be hidden vidcams," Raven said, looking both ways down the corridor they had emerged in. "Kez, find me a computer terminal now!"

Wraith was having no luck finding a flight of stairs anywhere in the maze of corridors. The laboratory had definitely been remodeled and he couldn't reorient himself enough to locate where the emergency stairs had been on the original plans. They might even have been blocked up by now. Twice they had run into security and had only got free by blasting their way through. That wouldn't work another time. The whole facility was on alert now.

Wraith also wasn't comfortable with killing so many people. But he had forced himself to accept that this was the cost of his sister's rescue. He rationalized that the scientists had killed thousands here over the years; more blood was on their hands than would ever be on his by killing them. But so much death revolted him and he was relieved that the gangers lacked his scruples. His comlink with Raven came to life—the private link rather than the unit he wore on his wrist.

"*We're three floors below you, Wraith,*" she told him. "*But we haven't found a terminal yet. It would seem the scientists put a lot of their findings on paper first.*"

"Keep looking," Wraith said aloud and in answer to a glance from Melek, explained: "Raven hasn't found a computer yet."

"*Watch your back, Wraith,*" his sister warned. "*I think there are hidden vidcams all over this place.*"

"Damn!" Wraith exclaimed. "Raven thinks we're being watched," he told the gangers. "We'd better find those stairs fast." There was a sudden yell from Finn as he pushed through a set of double doors ahead of them.

"Over here," he yelled back at them.

"Did you find the stairs?" Melek demanded as they joined him.

"Service elevator," Finn corrected, pressing the panel to summon the lift.

"Better than nothing," Wraith agreed. "Let's just hope they haven't locked down this one too."

His prayer went unanswered. The controls were covered by the same locking panel. This time it was Melek who went to work on it, while Wraith and Finn watched out for guards. Melek was using a laser to cut the panel off, a delicate task, as it could short-circuit the controls before they could use them. Wraith took advantage of an apparent lack of pursuit to contact Raven on his wrist com unit.

"Raven?"

"*Here,*" she answered immediately. "*No news yet, brother.*"

"That's not why I'm calling. Can you guess where Ali is? We've found another elevator and we need to know what floor."

"*One moment,*" Raven answered. "*I can locate her by her signal. Hang on . . . That's strange.*"

"What is?" Wraith demanded as Melek called out to him:

"Got it!"

"Good work," Wraith told him and he and Finn

squashed themselves into the elevator. Then he spoke into the com unit again: "Raven, I need a floor number."

"She's in another elevator," Raven told him, in tones of disgust. *"God only knows what the stupid kid thinks she's up to."*

"Raven!" Wraith shouted into the unit.

"OK, it's stopped. Five floors down," Raven told him. *"Now leave me alone. I have problems of my own."*

Wraith turned to Melek, but the ganger had already pressed the correct button.

"Sure hope there aren't more guards waiting for us down there," the ganger said fervently. "I don't know how long we can hold out."

"I know." Wraith's expression was set. "But Raven will take out that security system. We just have to give her time."

Ali had been nervous about using the elevator at night, certain that the scientists would detect an unauthorized use. But Tom had insisted that they try to get to Revenge before the gangers arrived. She wondered if his insistence had been partly motivated by the suspicion that, given the opportunity, Ali would leave him behind. She was annoyed by the thought that he didn't trust her, but admitted privately that he had grounds for suspicion.

The person she'd been only a month ago wouldn't have cared less what might happen to Tom. But the events of the last two weeks had changed her. From her encounter with Raven in the network to her capture by the CPS, forces had been in motion compelling Ali to reevaluate her conception of herself

and of everyone else. One of those forces had been
Wraith. His conviction that the extermination laws
were immoral had made her think for the first time
of what they actually meant to people besides herself. Her experience in the laboratory had brought
that home. She knew she wouldn't try to double-
cross Tom or Luciel. But they couldn't know that.

Whatever her misgivings, they seemed to make
the elevator trip unnoticed, arriving on the floor
where Revenge was without incident. The lights
were muted on all the corridors and they passed by
the rooms quietly.

"We should wake them up," Tom said at one
stage. "Get them ready to go."

"We'd better not." Ali shook her head at him.
"When my friends arrive they'll have enough problems without a bunch of kids all over the place."

"You're trying to get out of taking them," Tom ac-
cused.

"I'm trying to keep us alive," Ali hissed at him.
"And I won't do anything that could prevent our escape." *If I haven't done that already*, she added silently.

Luciel pushed open the door to Revenge's room
cautiously and in the dim light they saw a convulsive
movement from the bed.

"Who's there?" the girl demanded, her voice rising alarmingly, and Ali hastened to reassure her as
Luciel touched the panel by the door to activate the
lights.

"It's me," she said quickly. "Ali. We've come to
help you escape."

"There is no escape," Revenge told her and Ali

groaned inwardly. Obviously this wasn't one of the girl's lucid periods and she wondered how they would escape with someone more than half out of her wits.

"We're getting you out of here," she said as calmly as she could. "Raven's coming, remember?"

"Raven . . ." Revenge repeated, trying the word out.

"Ali," Luciel said softly, calling her attention to him. "She's still in restraints."

"I know." Ali frowned at them. "I just hope Wraith can do something about that. We'll have to wait until he gets here."

"He'd better get here soon or this escape will end in this room," Tom said gruffly. Then they all froze as a voice behind them replied.

"Your escape is already over."

Kez had run into the scientist as he searched one of the lab rooms and, before either of them had any time to gasp, Jeeva had grabbed the man and shoved him against the wall.

"Where are your computers?" he demanded. "Tell us or die!" The man looked wildly at the ganger, clearly terrified, as there was a soft laugh from behind them. Kez turned to see Raven raise an eyebrow at Jeeva.

" 'Tell us or die?' " she repeated.

"I can't tell you anything!" the scientist insisted. "We don't use computers!" Jeeva looked appalled, but Raven just shook her head, a nasty expression coming into her dark eyes.

"You're lying," she said softly. "You need equipment to process the results you get from the test-subjects. Where is it?"

"I don't know," the man moaned before Raven hit him hard with the butt of her pistol.

"Tell us *now!*" she insisted. "Or I'll let my friend kill you." Her eyes locked with those of the scientist for several long seconds. Kez's heart thudded at the look on her face. He'd never seen anything so utterly malevolent. Raven was clearly furious at the delay in their plans and every ounce of her anger was directed at the man she confronted now.

"It's over there," the scientist muttered, giving in to that cold stare.

"Show us," Jeeva told him, taking the initiative again and pointing the man in the direction he had indicated, setting his rifle against the scientist's back.

He was shaking with fear but led the way through the maze of corridors obediently. They seemed to have halted pursuit for the moment and Kez suspected that the guards were concentrating on Wraith's part of the team. But his suspicion proved false when they rounded the last corner and came face-to-face with six guards in CPS uniforms. Raven and Jeeva opened fire instantaneously, the ganger still holding the scientist in front of him as a human shield. Raven didn't have that protection, but before the guards could take advantage of that she'd retreated, pulling Kez after her. The resulting fire-fight lasted only five minutes. The guards were professionals, but they couldn't stand against the explosives Raven had devised. Within minutes the corridor was a blackened wreck and all six guards and the scientist were dead, the last an afterthought on Jeeva's part, annoyed by the man's earlier prevarication.

Raven crossed past the dead without blinking, stopping in front of a heavy door.

"This is what they were guarding," she said, kicking it experimentally. It swung open with a clang, the twisted metal attesting to the force of the explosives which had wiped out their opposition. Raven's eyes lit up as she saw what lay inside and Kez heaved a sigh of relief at the sight of the gleaming computer terminals.

"This is it, right?" Jeeva asked and Raven grinned at him.

"This is it," she confirmed. "Watch the door. This'll only take me a minute." With that she swung herself into a chair before one of the consoles and activated a terminal, seemingly at random. Kez stood at her side, watching her hands speed over the keypad before suddenly coming to rest as her eyes glazed over and she entered the computer system.

Ali turned around slowly, her companions following her lead. There was a hiss of rage from the bed as Revenge threw herself against her restraints, but the man who stood watching them ignored her. He was flanked by a detail of five armed CPS guards, but he wore a white lab coat over an expensive tailored suit. He didn't look like the kind of person who would inspire the obvious terror that gripped Tom and Luciel. He was white-haired and elderly, looking mild in comparison to the guards. Ali raised her eyes to meet his, and froze. A steel-blue gaze held her in place, seeming to turn her inside out and dispose of her in a few seconds.

"I don't think you're going anywhere," said the scientist she unhesitatingly identified as Dr. Kalden. "I was notified of an unauthorized elevator use on this floor. Would this escape of yours have anything to do with the group of vandals security has just disposed of?"

"Disposed of?" Ali paled in alarm and she heard Luciel gasp softly.

"It looks very like there's a conspiracy here," Dr. Kalden said, his eyes boring into Ali. "And I would very much like to know why you are attempting to remove this test-subject from the laboratory." He gestured toward Revenge casually and Ali glared at him. But before she could speak, Revenge beat her to it.

"She's coming for you!" she shrieked. "Raven's coming to wipe you clean with blood!"

"And who is Raven?" Dr. Kalden regarded Ali coldly. "Another of your ganger friends, Miss Tarrell? Or would she be another mutant?"

Ali didn't answer but she couldn't help an involuntary warning glance at Tom and Luciel, and that was all Dr. Kalden needed.

"I see," he said slowly. Then he turned to one of the CPS operatives. "Advise the rest of security that one of the terrorists is a mutant who will be aiming for the central computer room."

"Oh God," Ali groaned, transfixed with horror.

She'd betrayed Raven and now they were all going to die. She watched as the CPS guard reached for his com unit and then started as a new voice rang out.

"Drop it!" Wraith ordered, leveling his rifle at Dr. Kalden. Two sinister-looking gangers stood behind him, also pointing guns directly at the scientist.

"Wraith!" Ali thought she might faint from the sheer flood of relief that poured through her. "I thought they'd caught you!"

"Not yet," Wraith replied, keeping his eyes on the scientist. "What's going on here?"

"Your break-in has failed," Dr. Kalden informed him, unwavering despite the gun pointed at his head. "Give yourselves up."

"All I want is Ali and Rachel," Wraith told him. "Let them leave and you won't be injured."

The CPS operatives followed the conversation, their eyes going from one speaker to the other as they watched the stand-off. Ali had been watching as well, but now she felt she should say something. Wraith didn't know yet that he wouldn't just be taking two of them out. But it was then that Wraith got his first look at his sister.

"Rachel," he whispered, his eyes blank with grief. "Rachel, is that you?"

"Wraith?" For an instant the fury flinging herself against her restraints calmed, sanity returning. But the moment passed. "Let me free!" she screamed at Dr. Kalden. Wraith made a movement toward her, but was halted by the scientist's next words.

"Leave her," Dr. Kalden ordered. "It is *over*. You are outnumbered here, and your mutant friend trying to break into the control room will discover that our system is safe from any intrusion." He smiled chillingly. "There's a virus in that system which is activated automatically when the computers are accessed during a security alert. Your friend Raven won't get past that, however skilled she is."

As Raven allowed her mind to fuse with the laboratory's computer system she tried to concentrate on what her objectives were. Huge amounts of data surrounded her and the lure of those test results was hard to resist. But it was the security system she needed to find.

She flashed through the data streams, calling up information on the security alert. She was vaguely aware that the signals from Wraith and Ali's transceivers were getting closer and the information scrolling past informed her that they were about to be joined by two different security teams headed toward them.

> **cut power to elevators** < she commanded. > **lock out all access attempts not originating from this room.** < She was moving faster through the security database now, taking steps to terminate its effectiveness.

> **disrupt transmissions on frequencies used by CPS operatives** < she continued. > **cut transmissions from vidcams/motion sensors. cut power to electrified fencing** < Caught up in what she was doing, Raven issued her commands peremptorily, delighting in the way the computers obeyed her every whim. Valuable minutes had passed before she real-

ized that something was wrong. The system was slowing down, taking longer to carry out her orders, becoming sluggish. She tried to identify the cause of the problem and found it hard to focus. Her mind, wrapped around the circuitry, was subjected to the same blight as the computers. Raven tried to pull back some of the tendrils of her consciousness, realizing too late that the system was exercising a stranglehold on her, dragging her down into the depths of its own dementia.

Kez stiffened in alarm as Raven groaned, one hand slipping from the keypad as her eyes rolled back in her head. She was white, her brows drawn together in pain. As if on cue there was a shout from the doorway and the sound of gunfire. He heard the roar of Jeeva's gun and realized that there were more guards arriving.

"Raven!" he exclaimed, catching her arm and shaking it. "Raven! What's wrong?"

Wraith halted, the conviction in Dr. Kalden's voice turning him to lead. He was aware of what was happening but felt strangely divorced from it, overpowered by the realization of his own failure. He had convinced Raven to accompany him here; if he didn't surrender now he would lose her as he had lost Rachel; and Ali and Kez, dragged into something that had nothing to do with them, would die too.

"It's over," Dr. Kalden said again and Wraith lowered his weapon. It was time to end this. Suddenly there was an inarticulate cry of rage and frustration and Wraith blinked as one of the two boys who were standing with Ali launched himself at the scientist. One of the CPS operatives leaped to block him and they went down in a tangle of limbs, Dr. Kalden moving quickly behind his guards. A gun sprang into life as Finn took advantage of the distraction to attempt an escape, Ali screamed and then everyone was firing.

Wraith only had one object in view. He hurled himself across the room, blasting away the restraints that held Revenge down before overturning the bed and using it as a barricade to shelter her from the blazing guns even as he moved to face them, opening fire on a CPS guard. The fire-fight lasted a few more seconds, cut off as suddenly as it had begun. As Wraith stood he became aware of the sound of running footsteps and glanced at the door.

"It was the doctor," Ali told him, getting up from the floor, a cut on her forehead attesting that she had not been swift enough in seeking shelter. "He got away."

"Forget him!" Finn snarled, one arm hanging limply as he bent over his comrade.

"How is he?" Wraith asked, concerned.

"He's flatlined," Finn said harshly, using his good arm to reach to close Melek's eyes. "They got him."

"I'm sorry," Wraith began, when a movement recalled him to another casualty. He could see for himself that the boy was dead; blood streamed from the bullet wounds that had shattered his skull, staining the metal that encased his body. The second boy knelt at his side and Ali moved to help him up.

"Luciel, are you OK?" she asked.

"I'm OK," he told her, limping slightly as he stood. "I guess Tom would have wanted to go that way."

"What we gonna do now?" Finn asked, turning to Wraith, but it was not the ganger who answered.

From behind the bed a small ragged figure got to her feet, walking like an animated scarecrow. As they turned to look at her, Revenge croaked a response to Finn's question.

"Raven . . ." she said. "You must warn Raven."

"Raven!" Wraith's face darkened as he reached to flip on his com unit. "I hope it's not too late." He keyed to Raven's frequency and said her name urgently. "Raven, are you there?" There was a crackle and then a voice replied:

"Wraith, it's Kez! Something's wrong!"

"Where's Raven?" Wraith demanded.

"She's right here. But she's totally out of it, I can't make her hear me." Kez sounded frantic. *"And there are guards outside the room. I don't know how long Jeeva can hold them back!"*

"Stay with Raven," Wraith told him. "We'll try to get to you." But his heart sank at the thought. He doubted if they would get out of this facility alive.

A virus. Raven's thought processes finally connected enough for her to identify the source of the problem. Slowly a virus was shredding the computer system, endeavoring to take her with it. Well not this time. With the realization came rage. The fury crested within her as she realized that this had been something she hadn't anticipated and she took the first step to combat the threat. The million strands of her awareness snaked through the system, this time binding themselves to it, battling insanity with reason. Raven knitted the ravaged data streams back together, forcing them to mesh and become whole again.

The progress of the virus slowed under the onslaught of Raven's icy expertise. She controlled the system. Her conviction made it true. As the last trace of the virus disappeared she gradually became aware of other calls on her. Wraith was apparently attempting to use a deactivated elevator, Kez was shaking her insistently and someone was conducting a battle only meters away. Raven sent the command to unlock the elevator and turned to regard Kez.

"What happened?" she asked.

"You're back!" Kez's eyes were wide as he clutched her hand urgently. "I thought you were out for good."

"It would take more than an amateur computer virus," Raven said contemptuously, glancing back at the terminal.

"Is that what it was?"

"Yes. Do you have any more of those explosives?"

"No," Kez admitted. "I've used all mine."

"Take this then," Raven told him, producing a disc-shaped object from her pocket.

"What is it?" Kez asked, dubiously.

"A more powerful explosive," Raven said calmly. "Flip that switch, count to three, then throw it at the guards. Go now! I'm getting a headache from the noise."

Kez headed for the door and Raven grinned. Still keeping contact with the computer system, she used one hand to activate her com unit, setting it for wide receive so the rest of the team would hear her.

"Hey, Wraith! What's up with you?"

"Raven!" Wraith's voice came from her com unit, the relief in it evident. "Are you OK?" There was the sound of an explosion from the corridor outside, ringing in Raven's ears. She shook her head to clear it.

"I'm chill. You?"

"We've got Ali and . . . Revenge. But we've lost Melek."

"Damn." Raven frowned. "Get up here. We've got to move out soon."

"We'll be with you in a minute," Wraith replied.

As Raven cut the channel, Kez and Jeeva entered the room behind her. The ganger was wounded, his shoulder bleeding copiously, and he seated himself on one of the chairs to bind it up.

"I spoke to Wraith," Raven told him. "He said Melek didn't make it."

"Melek?" The ganger cursed under his breath, his expression dark with anger, but then shook his head. "There'll be time for that later—for now we've got to get out of this rat-trap!"

"Agreed," Raven replied. " But have you any idea how?" She indicated the computer terminal. "The CPS are crawling all over the place. I don't think we'll make it back to the flitter."

11

Blood Will Have Blood

Finn raised his gun warily as the elevator doors slid open, but this time there were no CPS guards waiting for them. Instead Kez stood on his own, holding a massive combat rifle that Wraith recognized as Jeeva's, his eyes wide and apprehensive.

"The control room's just down the hall," Kez said instantly. "We should get back there quickly before more guards turn up."

"Lead the way," Wraith agreed, lifting Revenge's emaciated figure into his arms. She was shaking, her eyes flickering wildly from one direction to another, but Wraith didn't have time to worry about her. Behind him Ali was supporting Luciel, whose limp had grown more pronounced, and Finn brought up the rear, keeping his gun trained on the empty corridor behind them.

Raven glanced up as they entered the control center and for a moment her gaze locked with Re-

venge's. The younger girl stiffened and Wraith released her, setting her down gently in one of the
empty chairs. As he did so Raven's attention moved
from Revenge to him.

"Wraith, we've got trouble," she said curtly.

"So I see," Wraith agreed, before looking back at
Finn. "Finn, Kez, you guard the door." He paused
while he looked at the boy Ali was supporting, then
added: "You, kid, can you handle a gun?" The boy
began to shake his head but Jeeva interrupted before
he could say anything.

"I'll go with them," the ganger said, retrieving his
combat rifle from Kez. Wraith nodded at him and
turned back to Raven.

"What's the stat?" he asked.

"This," Raven replied and all over the control
room screens sprang to life. They showed images of
the lab from monitors scattered throughout the facility, many of them focused on armed guards. Raven
hadn't moved, but her hands lay on a computer keypad, obviating the necessity. Clearly the computer
system was under her control. "I've restored some of
the lab's security programming," Raven explained,
"so we can keep track of the opposition."

"Do you know where the doctor went?" Ali
asked, joining them in front of the monitors.

"What doctor?" Raven frowned.

"Kalden," Ali's companion answered her. "He's
the senior research scientist here."

"He caught us in Revenge's room," Ali added, "but
then he got away before Wraith could stop him."

"I'll try to locate him," Raven said, "but right now

we have more important concerns." She paused and then added: "And who is this?"

"Luciel," Ali explained, looking guilty. "He's a friend."

"We were going to free the other test-subjects," Luciel said, his eyes meeting Raven's in a strange challenge.

"You're out of your mind," she returned. "We're going to have enough problems getting out of here ourselves, let alone bringing a bunch of kids with us."

The one thing that had sustained Ali while she was held in the laboratory was her knowledge of Raven's abilities. Although she trusted Wraith's promise of rescue, that promise could not have been made without Raven. When Dr. Kalden had claimed that Raven would fail to penetrate the lab's system, Ali had been shaken, but now she knew that Raven had succeeded, Ali's confidence in the younger Hex had increased. Now as Raven sat at the center of the control room, surrounded by flickering screens and the hum of machinery, Ali lacked the necessary conviction to promote her cause. But Luciel, who knew nothing of what Raven was capable of, felt no such restrictions.

"Have you any idea how many of us have died in this place?" he demanded of Raven, addressing her as the leader of the group in a recognition of the power she wielded within it. "How many more will die if you don't do something to help them? What kind of a rescue is this, if you only come for two out of the hundreds of us who are held here?" He paused before adding, in a quieter tone of voice: "A friend of mine was killed trying to help you people—doesn't that mean anything to you?"

"One of our team didn't make it either," Raven pointed out, still not turning away from her computer screens. "And I don't acknowledge the responsibility you're trying to make me feel." Her voice was cold and her eyes unreadable as she concluded: "Am I my brother's keeper?"

For a moment there was silence as Luciel struggled for words, and Wraith watched him as if waiting for a sign. Then from the side of the room a faint voice replied:

"You are his keeper as he is yours."

Wraith and Raven stiffened, before turning as one to look at Revenge, who returned their gaze with the impenetrability of an oracle. It was Wraith who broke that contact first.

"We must at least attempt to do something," he said.

Raven wrenched her gaze away from Revenge's and turned to glare at her brother, her black stare boring into him.

"We?" she queried. "You mean me, don't you? I've paid my dues, Wraith. You came here for Rachel and found Revenge. Now let's leave."

Kez shrank back behind the corner of the corridor as another burst of gunfire slammed into the wall. Jeeva swore under his breath before reloading his gun and angling it blindly round the corner to fire at the advancing guards. Kez glanced behind him. Twenty meters back was the open door of the control center and twenty meters behind that was another turn in the corridor, guarded by Finn. He too was firing round it, which meant more guards were coming in the other direction. Jeeva ducked his head round the angle of the walls and pulled back even faster.

"They're still coming," he told Kez, and articulated the boy's unspoken thought when he added: "We can't hold out much longer."

"Shall I tell Wraith?" Kez asked, gesturing to his wrist com unit.

"Go tell him in person," Jeeva replied. "Show him we're not kidding."

Kez didn't need any further persuasion. He swung round and raced back up the corridor and into the control room, coming to an abrupt halt as he realized an argument was in full force. Wraith and Raven were quarreling furiously, the girl having left her post in front of the computer keypad in order to argue her point more fervently. Ali and her friend were watching them anxiously, while keeping half an eye on the monitors which showed the advancing guards. Kez grabbed Wraith's arm.

"We've got to go now!" he insisted, ignoring the ganger's cold stare. "We can't hold out against the guards much longer."

"That's it then," Raven said. "We go . . . if we still can."

"If you leave now nothing will have changed," Ali's friend said softly. "The lab will just go back to normal, and the experiments will continue."

"Luciel!" Ali looked desperate. "There are *hundreds* of test-subjects. How do you expect us to break them all out, when we're having enough problems getting ourselves out?"

"So there are hundreds of people here," Luciel replied fiercely. "Have you any idea how many *thousands* have died as a result of the CPS's illegal experimentation, how many have—"

"Wait!" Raven commanded, and Ali and Luciel turned to look at her. "What did you say?" the girl asked, dark eyes fixed on Luciel.

"That there are thousands who have died," he replied. "Surely you know that?"

Raven had already turned away from him and faced Wraith. For the first time since the ganger had arrived she didn't look angry.

"The experimentation is illegal," she said in a considering tone of voice.

"So?" Wraith prompted.

"We can't take the test-subjects with us, but we can let other people know they exist," Raven replied. She turned and gestured to the computers. "This database is full of records of the test-subjects and the experiments performed on them. I can dump that information straight into the main net and into all the databases of the news channels. With a scoop like this the media will have people here in under half an hour."

"And you think that'll be enough?" Luciel challenged, still not looking convinced.

"It'll have to be," Wraith replied, having made his decision. He pressed two buttons on his wrist com unit and spoke into it. "Jeeva, Finn, can you hold on another fifteen minutes?"

"It's cutting it close, but it'll be chill," Finn replied, followed shortly after by Jeeva's voice agreeing.

"Right then," Wraith said, shutting his com unit off. "Get to it, Raven."

Three floors below the control center Dr. Kalden addressed a team of guards, while the scientists clustered in an alarmed huddle around him. A penetration of the facility alone might not have worried them, but the revelation that there was a rogue Hex on the loose had thoroughly frightened them. They were used to dealing with cowed children who barely understood what being a Hex entailed, let alone how to use those abilities. But now they knew that, not only were three of their test-subjects on the loose, the gangers had brought their own Hex with them.

"She must have broken past our virus safeguards," Kalden was saying angrily. "That means they're in control of the facility."

"There aren't that many of them, sir," one of the armed guards pointed out.

"There aren't that many of us either," a scientist said anxiously and Kalden frowned warningly.

"The intruders must be captured and disposed of," he insisted, "and do it quickly. If word of this gets out, there will be a number of awkward questions asked." A few of the scientists exchanged incredulous glances at the understatement, but most were too horrified by the possibility of discovery to do more than fix the remaining guards with hopeful eyes.

"We'll get them out of there, sir," the guard stated confidently. "A bunch of street trash and a few scruffy kids won't present any difficulty."

"They've already done that," Kalden said curtly. "Now get rid of them."

The security guards headed for the door, but Kalden halted them before they could leave.

"Wait," he ordered, his eyes narrowing to slits as he thought. "Leave the stranger, the Hex, alive if you can. I think she would make an ideal test-subject."

Raven stiffened at the words, a fragment of her consciousness alerting her to the conversation picked up by one of the monitors. One of her hands clenched slightly, but she didn't allow herself to become diverted from her purpose.

The laboratory's system was separated from all of the main information networks and she had almost given up hope of getting a message out. The communications lines were sealed against computer data flow, scrambling any signal sent out from the lab's computers. But there was one angle Kalden had failed to cover. It was a residential facility and the scientists required certain amenities. She had tracked the power grid to the residential area of the lab and discovered the vidcoms in almost every room. The vidcoms, used for recreation by the scientists, were configured to handle the data flow from the channels they picked up and send signals out in return. Raven tapped into that connection, and began rigging up a physical circuit in the control room to handle the jerry-rigged communication channel while she concentrated on the message she had to send.

She had no difficulty in finding convincing evidence of the CPS's illegal experimentation. From the moment she had destroyed the virus nesting within the system she had been downloading its data files. The duffel bag on the floor beside her was rapidly filling with disks. But in the course of her rape of the system she had located the evidence she would need, records of the experiments performed, complete from original assessments to final autopsy reports, coupled with a small but chilling selection of video recordings of some of the test-subjects. She patched the records together with the location of the lab, the identity of Dr. Kalden and the relevant section of European Law that allowed the extermination of Hexes and imposed the penalties for allowing a known Hex to live. There was no legislation precluding experimentation, but on that sub-clause alone, the CPS would find themselves with a lot of explaining to do.

The data package complete, Raven dived into her own connection with the network, and streamed toward the main UK directory. Tendrils of her consciousness snaked through the database, collecting listings of media channels, humanitarian organizations, government ministries and foreign embassies. She intended that this information dump would be as much of an embarrassment as possible to the government, which must have colluded in it. Her list complete, she added it to her information dump, so that those who received it would know exactly how widespread its release was.

> **send message** < Raven commanded and the system complied, sending out a thousand data pulses in every possible direction, arriving simultaneously in systems across the country.

The Hex's mouth tightened into a grim smile, but she wasn't finished yet. This time she was heading for the vidchannels themselves, tracking those streaming paths of data to their source. It was something she'd never tried to do before; the incompatibility of technologies would have made it difficult even when not operating from a separate system, but her use of those channels to send her message into the net gave her the idea of utilizing them more directly. As her consciousness ranged through each of the media vidchannels, leaving a tag on each, she directed the video monitors in the control room to pick up the feed from ten major channels, from news to entertainment. Then with a brief moment of intense concentration she pulled on those tags and released her data package.

Ali gasped as she saw what was happening. Ten of the monitor screens had been showing the images from vidchannels, apparently at Raven's command. But, just as she was about to inquire whether the other girl thought they were in need of some light entertainment, all the vidchannels blacked out for a microsecond, coming back on line simultaneously to show the same image. Pictures of mutilated children passed across the screen, covered by a continuously scrolling text, comprised of the test results. Test-subjects followed each other in rapid succession, each image accompanied by a name, details of the experiments performed and the date of death. Raven was flooding the vidchannels with proof that the world couldn't ignore.

As the others stared, Raven detached herself from the computer and turned to challenge Luciel with dark eyes.

"Satisfied?" she asked.

"Not entirely," he replied. "But it'll do."

"My pleasure," Raven bowed ironically and then turned to Wraith. "I'm going to bring the flitter to the roof of this building; we'll have to get up there some-how."

"Is that safe?" Kez asked, warily.

"How can you do that?" Ali demanded, their voices overlapping.

"I left the flitter's com-channel open. The scanning devices here don't pick it up as anything more than white noise, but if you know what you're look-ing for, and you have the skill, you can hack into its controls." She shrugged. "With running lights off, no one'll see it coming. But we can't afford to cut it much closer."

"Right," Wraith agreed and switched on his wrist com, broadcasting to Finn and Jeeva at once. "Get ready to make a break," he ordered. "The flitter will be waiting on the roof. We have to make it up there."

"OK, get ready to run then, friend," Jeeva's reply came back. "We won't be able to hold them here while we're heading in the opposite direction."

"Raven, can you control the lab system once we've left here?" Wraith asked sharply.

Raven reached into her coat and produced a small black control pad, which emitted a piercing sound, traveling quickly through the upper harmonics before disappearing from their hearing range. She held it in her left hand while her right hand traveled quickly over the keypad and then turned back to nod at Wraith.

"I can keep control for a while, but as soon as the scientists get back in here they can lock me out, *and* trace me by the signal from this."

"They'll be able to trace us anyway, once they've got their system back," Kez pointed out and Raven grinned at him.

"Not for long," she told them. "I'm setting an automatic domino circuit fuser. Once I trigger the right command this system will be irretrievably trashed."

"The data from the experiments will be lost?" Luciel asked.

"Unless they have copies," Raven replied. "But even if they lose it all, I've still got it."

"You downloaded the data files?" Luciel asked, wavering between surprise and disgust.

"The CPS have had access to these files for years," Raven pointed out. "It's about time a Hex got the chance." As she spoke she grabbed the last stack of disks and threw them into her bag. "I'm set," she told Wraith.

The ganger immediately switched on his wrist com and alerted Finn and Jeeva.

"Meet us at the elevator, one minute," he told

them. "We're getting out of here." Wraith slung the slumped form of Revenge over his shoulder and handed his gun to Ali. "Cover my back," he ordered and headed for the door.

"Wraith!" Ali's protest was almost a wail, but the ganger wasn't listening.

"Here," said Raven, coming up behind her. "Hold it like this." She adjusted Ali's hands on the weapon, placing one of them lightly on the trigger. "You see anything, shoot."

"But . . ." Ali began.

"It doesn't matter if you don't hit anything," Kez told her, reloading his own gun. "The guards won't charge into gunfire, and the important thing is to keep them back."

The CPS guards charged around the corner of the corridor as the sound of gunfire ceased, just in time to see the elevator doors close. The first man to arrive at the elevator pressed the call panel, but it was already dead.

"They're still in control of the system," he announced.

"But they're out of the control room," his leader responded. "Call Kalden and tell him this floor is secure. Have him get his scientists to release the lock on the elevators. Then get after the intruders."

Raven was jammed between Finn and Jeeva in the elevator, one hand gripping her customized gun, the other holding the link to the computer system. Through the transceiver she was aware of the computers still obeying her orders, pumping out the evidence over the vidchannels, locking out the security systems, transmitting all the data they had to Raven. She leaned against the hard white metal wall of the elevator, closing her eyes. They were burning with the pain of sensory overload and she could hear a buzz building up in her eardrums. Raven bit her lower lip hard, trying to concentrate on an easily defined pain, rather than the reality of what was happening to her. She had never engaged in so many complex computer operations at once. Now her body was finally feeling the strain and she knew that she was reaching her tolerance levels.

Slumped against the wall, trying hard not to succumb to the overwhelming flood of exhaustion, Raven didn't notice when the lift began to slow. But when it ground to a halt, Wraith grabbed her arm, shaking her roughly awake.

"Raven!" he demanded. "What's going on?"

"Wraith." Raven opened her eyes with an effort, not wanting to admit the truth. She concentrated and the elevator started again, the effort causing her knees to buckle. Kez caught her before she hit the floor and held her upright.

"Raven? You OK?" he asked, with concern.

"I'm fine," Raven insisted. She glared at him, but didn't pull away, admitting to herself, if not to her companions, that she lacked the strength to support herself anymore. She had been running on adrenaline and determination; now she had only the determination left. "We've got to get out of here soon," she told Wraith. "I won't be able to hold control over the computer much longer and I don't want to trigger the system wipe until we're safely out of the lab."

Dr. Kalden glanced angrily around the control room as he entered, and suddenly stopped dead. Behind him he heard a shocked gasp, but his consuming emotion was anger. Splashed across the row of security monitors were transmissions from vidchannels, their logos identifying them to be a broad section of the media. All of them were showing information so classified that only senior CPS officials had access to it.

"Our security has been compromised," he said in an icy voice.

"We'll be crucified," one of the scientists moaned and Kalden shot him a steely glare.

"This experimentation was authorized at the highest level," he stated. "If those gutter rats intend to accomplish anything by this, they are gravely mistaken." He studied the computer monitor for a few moments, then gestured to one of his operatives. "Shut down this transmission and get this system back under control. I want the lab's defenses back on-line now."

The operative seated himself at the terminal and his fingers sped rapidly over the keypad. After a few moments he began to frown.

"The system's acting up," he informed Kalden. "It's not letting me back in."

"She'll have put a block up," Kalden said impatiently. "Break it."

The operative returned to the keypad, watched intently by Kalden, and after a few minutes the images on the monitors winked out.

"I've shut down the transmission, sir," the man said with relief. "And I'm trying to regain control of the security system."

"Can you find out where the intruders are?" one of the guards asked. "If we know that we won't need the defenses—we can go and get them personally."

It was a while before the operative could persuade the computer system to provide him with an answer. Eventually he stated:

"They're on the roof."

"Get after them," Kalden ordered fiercely. "Don't let them leave this complex! That girl's been in this system—if she's allowed to escape she could do untold amounts of damage to our research."

As the security people raced after the gangers, one of the scientists turned to speak to Kalden:

"What if they escape, sir?" he asked nervously. "The media exposure alone . . ."

"There are ways to minimize this damage," Kalden said, cutting him off. "The media won't find anything here to use against us. I've taken precautions against that."

Wraith raced across the flat roof of the laboratory, still carrying the unconscious form of Revenge and closely followed by Ali and Luciel. Raven and Kez were a little behind them, Raven grudgingly accepting Kez's aid. Jeeva and Finn brought up the rear, guns ready for any sign of pursuit. The flitter was waiting for them and as they approached, the doors hissed open at Raven's command. Only Kez noticed her stagger as they did so.

Jeeva and Finn covered the area while Wraith placed Revenge as gently as he could in the back of the vehicle. He hurried Ali and Luciel in after her, retrieving his gun, and turned back to the others just as a shout rang out from across the roof.

"Guards!" warned Jeeva, and Finn spoke simultaneously:

"They've found us."

"I'm losing control of the system," Raven warned and the gangers ducked as the guards fired at them.

"Into the flitter!" Wraith ordered and Finn and Jeeva piled into the back as Raven took the driver's seat and Kez slid in beside her. Wraith fired one last volley at the guards, who were much closer now, before hurling himself inside, beside Finn. The doors hissed shut and the flitter took off into the air. Raven was using manual controls instead of her link with the machine, but even so the flitter climbed swiftly, out of the range of the guns and rifles.

"We're out of range," Finn stated and Ali breathed a sigh of relief. Two seconds later there was a flash of light and searchlights came to life all over the facility. There was the boom of an automatic gun and the flitter banked to avoid the fire.

"The CPS is in control of the computer system again," Wraith deduced. "Raven, kill it."

Kez turned to look at Raven as her eyes defocused, glazing over as she renewed her link with the lab's computer system. The searchlights went dead and the gun was silenced. Raven's eyes rolled up into her head and she slumped forward over the control panel, as the flitter went into a screaming dive.

"Raven!" Wraith yelled and Ali screamed piercingly. Kez lunged at the controls over Raven's body and forced the flitter back on course. He was shaking with tension as he wrestled with the controls, and climbed over Raven to pilot the flitter from the driver's seat.

"Can you handle it, kid? Jeeva asked and he nodded.

"Yeah, I think so."

"What's wrong with Raven?" Ali demanded, an edge of hysteria in her voice.

"She's still breathing," Kez assured her. "She must have knocked herself out shorting out that system."

"No sign of pursuit," Finn reported, from his vantage point at the back of the flitter.

"I think we're clear," Wraith responded. "Kez, what are you doing?"

"I can't pilot this thing without lights!" the boy replied angrily. "I'm not Raven. And if the Seccies caught us without lights on the road we'd be pulled over for sure."

"Stay chill," Jeeva told him. "Keep to the speed limit, follow the road. No one knows we were the ones who broke into that lab. There's no alert out yet."

"This place will be swarming with reporters in under an hour," Ali said authoritatively, losing a little of her tension. "We should worry about them as much as the Seccies, if we don't want to be caught on camera."

"When the media gets here Kalden will have a lot of explaining to do," Luciel said with satisfaction.

"I hope so," Wraith was beginning, when Finn gave a yell.

"Pursuit!" he warned. "Get off the road!"

Kez pulled the flitter aside, bringing it to a halt with a jerk and turning off the lights. It hovered there as the cause of Finn's warning became visible to the rest of them. A group of flitters with CPS symbols emblazoned on their side sped past them, not halting at all. In moments they were out of sight, but Ali pointed downward at more vehicles. Skimmers were on the road below them, heading away from the lab at high speed.

"The scientists," Luciel said softly.

"Rats deserting a sinking ship," Ali added.

"I don't like this." Wraith's voice was grim as he watched the lights fade into the distance.

"I guess they don't want to be here when the media arrive either," Kez said, craning back to look in the direction of the laboratory.

It was out of sight, no lights left to show them its location. But all six watched apprehensively, infected by Wraith's foreboding.

And then they saw it. The light of the fireball reached them before the sonic boom of the explosion. Clouds of smoke and fire boiled into the sky, throwing flaming debris high into the air. Then the shockwave hit them and the flitter rocked with the air disturbance as the ground far below shook. Wraith clenched his fists and Ali hid her head in Luciel's shoulder but no one spoke as Kez guided the flitter back over the road, heading back to London while the fireball lit the sky behind them.

12

Lies Like Truth

The vidscreen was on. It had been on constantly for the past three days since their escape from the lab. Ali sat on the floor of the squat, in front of the battered unit, not looking at any of the others. Barely a word had been spoken since they had arrived back in London, after the long, weary night, and negotiated with the Countess for the use of one of her properties. It was down in the depths of London, in precisely the setting that would in other circumstances have frightened Ali and annoyed Raven. But no one was complaining.

Raven hadn't stayed with them. Wraith had told her about the destruction of the lab but she hadn't said much in response, white and tired from overstraining herself, except to ask if Kalden had escaped. No one knew the answer and when Kez suggested she link up to the net Raven had just shook her head. Once they reached London she had stated her intention of seeking sanctuary with the Countess and no one had had the energy to argue with her.

The others had been isolated in the three rooms that comprised the squat. Jeeva and Finn had returned once for their payment and to tell Wraith that their gang would not be exacting retribution for Melek's death. Luciel had remained, tinkering with the electronic equipment that Raven had abandoned when she'd disappeared into the Countess's fortress-like building. He didn't speak much, burdened by the weight of his guilt for the lives that had been lost when the lab was destroyed. Wraith was also silent. He spent long hours caring for Revenge, trying to coax a resemblance to the child he had known out of the shattered body of the test-subject. Ali already knew that the effort was wasted. But Wraith was trying to salve his own conscience by caring for the child he had managed to save. Kez was still with them, but he disappeared for long hours at a time, wandering the streets of the urban catacombs.

The group had fragmented and Ali blamed it on the absence of Raven. Wraith and his sister had balanced each other, his private humanity providing a foil for her public ruthlessness. Together they had been the perfect leader. His caution and her daring had carried them through the raid on the lab, but having achieved that end the link had been lost. Ali suspected Raven would have disappeared anyway, whatever had happened; the presence of Revenge disturbed her on a level that made it difficult for her to remain. Unlike Wraith, she had never once called her sister by her old name, a tacit recognition of the change that had overtaken her. But the presence of Revenge was not the only reason for the fragmentation of the team. That had come inevitably with the sense of failure that had overtaken them all, once the media coverage had begun.

The appearance of the lab records on every main vidchannel simultaneously had stunned the media as much as the general public, and reporters had been immediately dispatched to the alleged location of the CPS facility. The footage they had sent out had appeared within the hour on every major news channel, showing the gutted shell that had been the lab. But before the reporters could examine the wreckage the Security Services had arrived, with a government injunction, forcing the media to leave. The news channels had continued to speculate on the situation over the next day and their persistence had been rewarded with the announcement of an official investigation. The government had stubbornly refused to comment and despite the inevitable comments from sources it became clear that officialdom was stonewalling the media.

The team had watched this from the relative safety of the squat with increasing frustration. Raven had regained consciousness after twelve hours and refused all offers of medical treatment to watch the vidscreen. But she was the first to turn away from the coverage, announcing that she was going to see the Countess and declining Kez's company on the way. Finn and Jeeva had left shortly afterward, declaring that their part of the operation was over.

Jeeva had wished them luck, but Finn had departed without a word, impatient to call an end to their association.

Wraith had lost interest in the coverage in the light of Revenge's continuing vacancy. Luciel had done his best to explain what had happened to her and to assist Wraith in taking care of her. But the girl had retreated into her own mind. Her periods of lucidity were rare and came in the middle of incoherent ravings, so that Ali could never be certain at what point reality began for her. She had nightmares too, and after waking three nights in a row to the sound of banshee screaming, Ali's own dreams were displaying the same maelstrom of insanity. Flames licked at her, while the screams rang on, sleeping and waking. She would have left too, but unlike Raven and Kez, or even the gangers, she had nowhere to go. She and Luciel were trapped there by the simple fact that any of their old connections would refuse to aid them. As far as their parents were concerned, they were dead, and Ali reflected that the way things were going that was likely to come true before very much time had passed.

Wraith could hear the muted sound of the news channel, even through the closed door. He wished Ali would turn the thing off, but she had seemingly taken root in front of the screen and only removed her gaze with reluctance. At least her obsession with the coverage was preferable to her wandering around the squat, mournfully regarding all she saw as if she were interred in a tomb. Wraith sympathized with her situation, but he didn't feel himself equal to handling it. It was difficult enough to come to terms with the fact that his long search for his sister was over, without the satisfaction of having really found the object of that search. Revenge was an entirely alien creature to him, and he could see little or nothing of what he had lost in the shadows of her haunted eyes.

She was sleeping again, a natural sleep, if disturbed by the dreams that plagued her, and Wraith took the opportunity to check on Ali.

"What's happening?" he asked as he entered the room, gesturing at the scratched screen.

"There's going to be an official statement this evening, given by the Prime Minister, followed by an announcement by the Head of the Security Services. Most of the news channels are speculating on what they'll say, some are rerunning the transmission from the lab, to see if they can detect any evidence of fraud."

"Has that been suggested?" Wraith asked.

"There's been a lot of claims that the data from the experiments and the pictures of the test-subjects were fabricated by Hexes in an effort to gain public sympathy. But people don't believe that explanation because the government claims that no Hex can get past the ever-vigilant CPS." Ali's voice was bitter, and Wraith couldn't blame her. It hadn't been that long since her own exposure as a Hex, and unlike Raven she hadn't had time to come to terms with the revulsion in which mutants were held.

If Raven were there she might have made it easier

for Ali. Wraith was aware of the mutual antipathy between them, but none the less Raven might have been able to help Ali come to terms with her new identity as a member of the criminal under-classes. Perhaps she could even be taught how to use her Hex abilities to survive on the streets. Wraith found it difficult to imagine Ali as a hacker, but she hardly had an abundance of opportunities on offer. However, Raven had disappeared, and he didn't know if she ever planned to return.

Kez crossed the bridge with care. This far down most of them were ruined. The essential base structure of the city was secure, but the government hadn't spent money on the upkeep of areas inhabited primarily by criminals. The area where the squat was located was further down than the depths where Kez had spent his childhood. He rarely saw gangers, who hunted the poorer suburbs where pickings were better. Instead the few people he saw wandering the deserted bridges and ruined plazas were society's unwanted, those who had given up hope.

He wandered on listlessly, wondering if this was where he belonged. He didn't know what Wraith intended to do, whether he would go back to Denver or join up with the gangers here. Perhaps he would rely on Raven to provide sufficient credit for him to live in obscurity, taking care of Revenge. If that happened, Kez would have little choice but to return to the streets. He had effectively blocked out the memory of his former life; now he felt it returning to claim him. Everything depended on Raven. He was certain of it. Without her, the team was nothing. Her expertise, her ruthless exploitation of her abilities, had given them confidence in her as the main power of the group.

Without realizing it, he had come to familiar territory. The building that loomed beside him was the one where the Countess had her base of operations, three levels up. That was where Raven had been headed when she left them. Kez studied it blankly, wondering if he dared. Then, deciding that he had nothing to lose, he began to climb the stairs that snaked around the skyscraper.

The guards in the foyer looked up warily as Kez entered, and moved to block the door that led up to the Countess's base of operations. He approached with equal caution, but the request he made when he reached them was unexpected.

"I want to see Raven," he stated.

The guards looked at each other, then the woman frowned in consideration.

"The hacker?" she asked.

"Yeah, that's her," Kez confirmed. "I heard she was here."

"Wait," the woman said coldly, and turned to speak into the vidcom, too quickly for Kez to make out her words. Finally she stepped back from the unit and gestured him forward. "State your name and business."

Kez didn't know if Raven was at the other end of the vidcom or not. But he assumed that the message would be passed on to her and spoke as if she was there.

"It's Kez," he said. "I need to talk to Raven. It's important."

"Is it personal business?" an unfamiliar voice asked, and Kez nodded. "Wait there," the voice responded and the vidcom clicked off.

"You heard her," the male guard told him. "You can wait over there." He waved Kez away from the door and both guards resumed their alert stance.

Long minutes passed as Kez waited. There was no sign of Raven, and the guards were ignoring him. He wondered if he had made a mistake in coming here. But the compulsion to see Raven had been too strong for him to resist. One of the guards shifted and the motion drew Kez's eyes to the open doorway just as a figure emerged from the shadows. Raven was dressed simply in black, her hair scraped back to reveal her pale face and the dark shadows under her obsidian eyes. She was wearing her duffel bag slung over one shoulder and carrying her long coat and Kez let himself hope for the first time since the lab had burned to the ground.

"Hey, Kez," she said as he approached. "What's up?"

"Not much," he admitted. "Everyone's just ..." He shrugged his shoulders, completing the thought with the gesture.

"Fallen apart," Raven concluded. For a moment a brief flicker of something passed across her face and was gone before Kez could identify it. "What did you expect?" she shrugged. "Did you think everyone would be on a high because we'd found Rachel? It's not that easy, Kez. Wraith hasn't won a war, or even a

235

battle, whatever he might think." She shook her head. "In the real world no one lives happily ever after; it's hard enough just to keep living." Kez said nothing and after a moment Raven adjusted the strap of her bag and began to walk off. "Come on, let's go."

"Back to the squat?" Kez asked, falling into step with her.

"For now," Raven answered.

She had been following the news broadcasts when Kez arrived, listening to the speculation about the Prime Minister's statement. Admittedly, that statement was probably already written and lying in some government database, safe from any but the most electric of hackers. But Raven hadn't entered the net since the night of the raid. Her time had been spent with the data files she had extracted from the lab's computer.

The data on those disks had been collected from the results of sadistic experiments performed over more than fifty years, on thousands of children. But Raven had forgotten that as she read the files. She wanted to know what it meant to be a Hex, what the scientists had discovered. But she learned more about what they didn't know than what they did. Raven had always known that she was unusual. She had known she was a Hex long before any government agency could have guessed and learned to use her talents before she really understood what they were. But, reading through the CPS's files, she realized the flaw in their ruthless policy of exterminating mutants as soon as they were discovered. The test-subjects had no idea what they were capable of and, consequently, neither did the scientists. Some of the research had yielded useful results, but most of it consisted in dead-end and blind-alley projects which seemed to miss the point entirely. Dr. Kalden's team had never encountered anyone with abilities that came anywhere near to matching Raven's; the virus they had constructed within their computer system to catch a Hex hacker had told her that. If she could evade the best defenses the lab had, at her age, a more experienced Hex ought to be able to do far more. Raven wondered if any more experienced Hexes even existed, then dismissed the question. The main concern was that she existed and as long as she continued to extend her skills they would surpass any possible expectation of the CPS researchers.

Raven grinned silently. Her experience in the lab had been sobering. She'd never suffered the sensory overload of extended connection with the net before. But, once she had recovered from the experience, the realization that she was just as much of a threat to the CPS as they were to her had reassured her. She felt her confidence building as they approached the squat where the others waited and her grin didn't fade as Kez opened the door.

Ali glanced up idly as the door opened, and her eyes widened with shock as she saw who it was.

"Raven!" Wraith said, affection and relief in his voice. "How are you?"

"I'm chill," Raven grinned at him. "I see you've

made yourself comfortable," she added, glancing iron-ically around the bare room. "Makes a change from the Belgravia Complex, doesn't it?" This last was ad-dressed to Ali, who blinked, uncertain whether it was intended to indicate malice or camaraderie. "Have you been watching the screen all this time?" Raven contin-ued, dumping her bag and coat and seating herself against the wall.

"Pretty much," Ali admitted cautiously. "Wraith's been looking after . . ." she hesitated and Raven fin-ished for her:

"Revenge." She turned to look at Wraith. "Any improvement?"

"No," he stated flatly.

"I didn't expect there would be," Raven replied.

"I bet you don't even care either," Luciel stated from the corner of the room, where he had been sit-ting, virtually ignored. His voice was just as cool as Raven's. "You didn't even see the lab explode."

"I've seen the news reports," Raven reminded him. "And I'm not flagellating myself with guilt. Tell me one thing we could have done that we didn't," she challenged. "Just one."

Luciel met her eyes for a long moment, but he didn't speak. Raven held his gaze and then turned away toward the door of Revenge's room. Wraith was the only one to follow her and as they went in-side, he shut the door behind them. Revenge was sleeping, her fragile body collapsed on the bed like a broken doll. Raven studied her for a while in silence until Wraith spoke.

"Will she recover?"

"You know the answer to that as well as I do," Raven replied. Turning her back on Revenge she continued: "Was she worth it? Was finding Rachel that important to you?"

"She wasn't to you?" Wraith replied, his words half question, half statement.

"As Luciel said, hundreds have died. Does the fate of one more Hex make any difference?"

"If you care about hundreds, you have to care about one," Wraith said quietly. "How much do you care, Raven?"

Before Raven could answer him, they heard Ali calling and the sound of the vidscreen being turned up. Raven turned away to join the others and, after a few seconds, Wraith followed her to the next room where the coverage of the Prime Minister's statement was beginning.

"Tonight George Chesterton, the Prime Minister, will address the House to make a public statement on the recent allegations concerning the Center for Paranormal Studies, the UK body responsible for the elimination of defectives with the mutant Hex gene."

"Defectives?" Ali exclaimed and Luciel hushed her.

"Get used to it," Raven said dryly, not looking away from the screen.

". . . now we go live to the British Parliament, where Mr. Chesterton is about to make his official statement."

The scene shifted to the circular parliament building where a tall man with graying hair was regarding the house with an expression of severe authority.

"Honorable and right honorable members, I come here

239

tonight to quell the speculation concerning the integrity of this government and to speak out against acts of terrorism such as those inflicted upon the British people last week. The invasion of a CPS extermination facility, the fabrication of records from that facility, the publication of those records and eventual destruction of the facility concerned are all acts of astounding terrorism, perpetrated by a group of criminals sympathetic to the cause of illegal mutants. Rest assured these criminals will be caught. In the meantime I would like to state categorically that I have every confidence in Governor Charles Alverstead, the current head of the CPS, and in his operatives, including the head of the facility, who was hospitalized last night after injuries sustained during a valiant defense against the terrorists. His courage and heroism are an example to us all."

The Prime Minister seated himself to cheers from all over the house, and the news reporter broke in on the footage to state that a short announcement by the Head of the Security Services would follow. They all watched the screen in appalled fascination as the cheering continued in Parliament. Kez was the first to speak.

"They're all in on it!" he exclaimed. "It's all being covered up."

"Will the public fall for it?" Wraith asked, turning to Raven, but it was Ali who answered him.

"I'm sure they will," she said. "People will want to believe it. Everyone knows that Hexes are criminals and those pictures of the experiments were hard to take." She swallowed. "Some people might doubt, but not enough of them to sway public opinion."

"She's right," Raven agreed. "I have a great deal of faith in human nature—they'll believe it."

"Every word of it is a lie," Luciel said, but no one replied. The uniformed figure of the Head of the Security Services had just appeared on the screen. He began his announcement without ceremony.

"The Security Services have identified several of the participants in the raid on the CPS facility. Descriptions and artists' impressions follow. If any citizen has been contacted by these people please inform the Security Services immediately. They are terrorists, known to be killers, and all are believed to be armed and dangerous."

Ali's eyes widened in amazement as the screen filled with pictures and statistics.

"Suspect One: Wraith, young male with prematurely white hair and gray eyes, about average height. Suspect Two: young male with dyed blue hair, and green eyes, believed to be of Irish descent. Suspect Three: Caucasian boy with blond hair and brown eyes. Suspect Four: Raven, young female, known to be a rogue Hex."

The item ended with another plea for anyone with information on the terrorists to come forward, and then the reporter's image appeared on the screen as a panel of hastily assembled political analysts began to discuss the situation over vidcom links. The discussion opened with the reporter asking why mutant sympathizers were engaging in terrorist acts now, when the extermination laws had been enacted 269 years ago.

The vidscreen went dead as Raven leaned forward to turn off the unit and they regarded each other in the sudden silence.

"Why didn't they mention me or Luciel, or Revenge?" Ali asked eventually.

"Because legally you're dead," Raven pointed out. "The CPS have records of your extermination; they can hardly admit that you are alive without confirming the reports of the experiments."

"You're still in danger," Wraith stated. "They may not be admitting to it, but I'm certain the Security Services know exactly who you are."

"There wasn't a description of Raven," Luciel pointed out.

"No one saw me and lived to tell," the girl said grimly. "Jeeva flatlined them all." Then she glared at the screen. "But I've never been this visible before. The CPS never even knew I existed. Now they know my name and they know how much of a threat I am."

"Are you intending to go to ground?" Wraith asked, knowing that such an action would be uncharacteristic for Raven.

"Are you?" she asked.

Wraith considered, aware that all eyes were focused on him. He thought about the extermination laws, about the things he had seen in Kalden's laboratory, about the broken body of Revenge and about Raven's continual fight to stay alive. Finally he remembered the official denial, the lies that would be believed unless the government could be forced to acknowledge the immorality of what they were doing and had done ever since the Hex gene was first created. The hopelessness of the past few days was erased as he made his decision.

"No," he stated. "I'm not going to hide."

HEX

"What then?" Raven asked, with a strange expression in her eyes.

"I'm going to fight it," Wraith declared. "The government thinks we're a threat, so let's *be* a threat."

"Become terrorists?" Ali asked.

"No." Wraith shook his head. "Don't let them label us that way. Thousands have died because of their lies already. Whatever you do, you mustn't believe them." He paused to study them each in turn. Luciel, Ali, Kez, Raven and the closed door of the room where Revenge lay sleeping. "Think of what we've accomplished already," he told them. "I think we should stick together."

They looked at him. Ali's eyes were shining with hope, and Kez and Luciel were smiling for the first time since the raid. It was a responsibility that Wraith had not intended to take on. But since he had arrived in London every step had led him inexorably toward the conclusion that this was something he *had* to do. But he knew as well as the rest of them that the decision was not entirely his to make. They would follow him alone if necessary, but as he turned to look at Raven, he sensed their eyes follow his.

Raven's head was bent, her eyes hooded as she thought. They waited for her answer, knowing that while Raven would never consent to hide, agreeing to fight was quite another thing. Then she raised her head and grinned wickedly. With an exuberant gesture she shook her hair free from its confinement and stood up.

"I'm with you," she said. "It should be wild."

* * *

The flitter rose slowly through the levels of London, piloted by a dark-eyed girl whose hands rested lightly on the controls. No one noticed them as they cruised past the bridges, a Security Services skimmer remained stationary as they flew over it, keeping to the speed limit. Three levels further up Raven turned to the figure in the passenger seat and raised an eyebrow quizzically. Kez looked back slyly, conscious of Wraith seated behind them.

"Dare me?" Raven asked.

"Go for it," Kez replied and the flitter went into a screaming climb. Raven's laughter was drowned out by the music that blasted from the flitter's speakers as they swept out of London, heading for the sky.

About the Author

RHIANNON LASSITER is a graduate of Oxford University. The first literary agent to see her work encouraged her to finish *Hex*, which she wrote when she was seventeen, and it was immediately bought by the first publisher who read it. Her mother is a well-known children's author, and she lives in London.

As well as writing, Rhiannon runs her own web-design business, writes articles and reviews of children's books, and is part of the production team Armadillo, a children's books review publication. Her other interests include computer and role-playing games, watching films, reading, rollerblading, and seeing her friends.

Hex: Shadows and *Hex: Ghosts* are also published by Simon & Schuster Children's Division.